LETTING GO

OF THE PERFECT

Jacob's Story

ALSO BY SAVASLAS LOFTON

FICTION

At a Mirror's Glance

Praise for At a Mirror's Glance

I recently ordered the book "At a Mirror's Glance" and began reading it. I just finished it this morning, and I must say it was tough for me to put down. I am a very avid reader, and I just love it when I find a book I can't put down. The book was so detailed that it was easy to picture each scene as it was described. God has blessed this author with so many amazing and incredible talents. When is the next book coming out? I can tell you now that I will be one of the first to read it. - *Brandi D.*

Tilts glasses Ok, so I love the book! It was absolutely a joy to read. I love the different literary devices you used to tell the story, such as imagery and foreshadowing. I also enjoyed that you were able to write it from a male and female perspective. I absolutely loved the characters, from the gossiping lady in the salon to Frank's drama. All of them reminded me of people I know or have known at one time or another. I'm looking forward to the next. I'm going to pass the word on to my friends!! - *Kymon C.*

This book was beautifully written, the characters were relatable, and the story was captivating and engaging. It kept me turning the page from the very beginning. This book's depiction of love was simple, elegant, and realistic. If you are looking for a great, easy read that will have you turning the page until the last word, check out this book. - *Walter S. III*

I just finished reading "At a Mirror's Glance" by Savaslas Lofton, and I want to encourage all of you to purchase this book! I love to read, and as a writer, I love a story that engrosses me... whenever I had to set the book down, I found myself wondering what would happen next in Lisa's life! I laughed... cried... felt discouraged... and was even ministered to throughout the novel. It is a book about real stuff and real people's encounters. I hear another novel is coming, and I will be waiting... excellent book! - *Yolanda S.*

WOW!!! What an amazing story!!! I have purchased 6 books in the last 2 months, and this novel is the first one I have read from beginning to end in one day!!! Author Savaslas Lofton did a fantastic job of keeping the suspense coming while delivering an important and powerful message about finding true love and appreciating it when it comes along.

This novel has changed my life and perspective on love for the better! This is a movie in the making!!! – *SoulChic*

Charles Newman Jr.

March 12, 1962 – September 24, 2022

I dedicate this novel to the cherished memory of Elder Charles Newman Jr., a spiritual big brother who left an indelible mark on my life of encouragement, brotherhood, and support. I would also like to extend my gratitude to his wife, Mrs. Caryn Newman, for allowing me this great honor of dedicating this book as a token of love to the Newman family.

Faith is not about perfection, but surrender. Healing does not arrive with certainty, but with trust. And sometimes, **love** *is God's way of asking us to loosen our grip, so we can finally be held.*

— Savaslas Lofton

Author's Letter

In *At a Mirror's Glance*, Lisa Williams believes strength is found in control of her choices, her emotions, and her carefully curated life. She is accomplished and driven yet quietly carries the grief of losing her father and the spiritual certainty she once trusted to guide her heart. Her checklist for love is not born of vanity, but of self-preservation, a way to keep disappointment and God at a manageable distance.

Jacob enters her life not as a flawless answer, but as an unexpected invitation. He is steady where she is guarded, faithful where she is fearful, and unwilling to perform for approval. He does not meet the standards Lisa created to feel safe, yet he embodies the grace she never learned how to receive.

Letting Go of the Perfect returns to this story years later, this time through Jacob's eyes. It explores the quiet courage required to lead with humility, to choose obedience over impulse, and to love deeply without recognition.

Prologue

In Which Certainty Fails

I met Lisa after she had learned to be careful.

By then, she had already lost the one thing that once steadied her, though she rarely spoke of it. Grief does not always announce itself as sorrow. Sometimes it arrives as discipline, precision. A belief that if you choose correctly enough, nothing else will be taken from you.

She believed this.

And for a while, *so did I.*

Lisa evaluated love the way she evaluated risk: quietly, thoroughly, with rules that left little room for error. I did not meet the most important of them. That should have been the end of it. Instead, it was the beginning. What followed looked, from a distance, like order. Marriage. Work that mattered. A child who arrived early and stayed. We built a life that suggested stability, and I mistook it for permanence.

I've spent most of my adult life believing in direction, morality, spirituality, and community. I lead. I counsel. I speak with conviction about endurance. But I was learning that conviction does not prevent fracture; it only delays it.

The first crack came quietly.

A pregnancy complicated by uncertainty. A rumor whose origin mattered less than its effect. And a memory, uninvited, returning with questions I had never allowed myself to ask. I found that the faith I offered so freely to others became harder to find in myself.

Lisa once learned that perfection was an illusion.

I was learning that belief can be one too.

This is not a story about collapse. It is a story about what remains when the scaffolding falls away.

Chapter 1

1983

"And life for me ain't been no crystal stair."

Langston Hughes

My mother and I lived in a two-bedroom, olive-green shotgun house on the northeast side of Dallas. All the furniture was second-hand.

Mustard yellow. Cherry red. Orange suede.

Nothing matched.

Each piece carried a story, old couches and chairs,

dressers and mirrors that had already belonged to someone else. And somehow, among all those inherited histories, there was still room for one lasting story.

Ours.

Late eighties summers turned the house into a furnace. By midafternoon, the air soured, thick with a musty heat rising from cracked plastic tiles and worn red carpet that ran like a faded ribbon down the narrow hallway. We pushed portable fans into the windows and waited for mercy.

Most days, it didn't come.

On my mother's rare days off, we rode the transit bus downtown. Even exhausted, she lifted herself from the mattress with quiet resolve. She never complained. She moved more slowly, conserving what little strength she had left, as if energy, too, needed to be budgeted.

We strolled past boutique windows. Mother lingered longer than she realized, her reflection caught between draped in silk and summer linen. Wanting, even *briefly*, felt like a luxury.

I reached into my pocket and pulled out a crumpled dollar bill I had found on the curb earlier that day.

"Mother," I said softly, holding it up, "is this enough to buy you that pretty dress?"

She smiled, a smile that carried both tenderness and

truth.

"I don't think so, baby. But that's alright. One day, you'll buy me all the dresses you want after you graduate college and land that dream job."

She folded my fingers gently back over the dollar, pressing my hand closed as if sealing something more than currency, as if pressing faith into my palm.

I slipped the bill back into my pocket and tucked her words somewhere deeper, where promises are kept safe.

We always ended our trips at my favorite place: the library. That's where my love for reading began, between tall shelves and quiet corners that felt cooler than the rest of the world.

On the way home, we stopped at a corner store for my orange push-up ice cream, its bright sweetness cutting through the heat.

When summer became unbearable, we sat on the porch beneath a wide shade tree that offered just enough relief to keep us upright. Even there, the air carried a faint trace of industrial fumes from nearby factories.

My mother lowered herself into her chair and fanned her face with a stack of overdue bills. The paper bent and fluttered in her hand like something trying to escape. Each wave stirred the air but changed nothing. We were held in place by circumstances that did not loosen easily.

I escaped the only way I knew how, on my bike.

I rode until sweat soaked through my shirt, stopping only long enough to drink from the outside faucet of water before racing back into the street for handball, dodging cars that never bothered to slow down.

When evening finally softened the heat, I drifted home guided by the crackle of my mother's records playing through the open window, music spilling into the dusk like reassurance that we were still here.

Her music collection was vast. But *Thriller* was everything.

Michael Jackson's red leather jacket from the "Beat It" video lived rent-free in my imagination.

Since owning one was impossible, I made my own using one white sock, Elmer's school glue, and glitter. That glove permitted me to believe I could become something *more*. I practiced every kick, every spin, every slide until the concrete beneath my feet became a stage.

One afternoon, while rehearsing for the middle school talent show, a man passing by slowed near our rusted chain-link fence.

"Hey, kid," he said, watching for a moment. "Looks like you've been studying MJ. Not bad."

"Thank you," I replied, cautious but polite.

He leaned against the fence. "Would you believe me if I told you someone who played with Michael Jackson lives right here in this neighborhood?"

"No way," I stepped closer.

"You've probably already seen him," he continued. "Might've even walked right past him."

My fingers wrapped around the metal links. "Who?"

"Ever heard of *Music Man?*"

"The drunk old guy?" I asked. "The one always talking to himself? Moving his hands like he's playing something that isn't there?"

The man nodded. "He was a saxophonist. A real one. Good enough that if he hadn't been touring Switzerland with his jazz band, he might've played in Michael's band."

The idea unsettled me: greatness existing just blocks away from struggle, with talent breathing the same heavy air we did.

"Lost it all to drugs and alcohol," he added.

He looked somberly down at the ground, and shook his head in empathy. He continued, "He ended up broke. Homeless. Right here on the streets of Eagle Ford."

At that moment, I had no idea how closely music, hunger, and violence would come to share the same address in my life, or how talent and ruin could emerge from the same soil.

Chapter 2

Music Man

I sat on the cracked concrete of the porch. My arms folded over the peaks of my knees, waiting for *Music Man*, the fallen musical hero of Eagle Ford, to walk by. Now that I knew the background of his story, anticipation churned in my chest, sparking restless hope. But as the hours crawled by, my excitement twisted into disappointment and impatience. I felt an urge to escape to the park for a quick game of pickup tackle with some neighborhood kids, craving distraction.

Just then, I heard chanting, mocking like a King's proclamation: "*Music Man, Music Man...* here comes *Music Man*! He's crazy! He even smells like dog poop!"

The boys followed him on their bicycles, circling like vultures. Their words sliced through the air. Anger flooded me before I could stop it.

Music Man's clothes were caked in dirt and streaked with old oil, but I saw beyond the grime. He moved to a rhythm only he could hear, hands shaping invisible notes. Untouched by their cruelty. Or pretending to be.

Shame pricked my skin, burning hot, for sitting still while their laughter swelled into a cruel chorus. I froze as they hurled rocks.

One struck him on the side of the head, causing him to bleed from the top of his temple.

He stumbled. The broken grocery cart carrying everything he owned tipped and clattered onto the pavement beside him. Something inside me snapped, my fists clenched, heart throbbing tight against my ribs, panic and fury colliding. I shouted, stepping toward the fence, "Leave him alone! He's not bothering anyone!"

Antonio turned.

"Come say that to my face, and I'll punch you, punk!" His fists were already clenched.

Antonio led a small gang in the neighborhood, boys eager to prove themselves. The ones who passed his tests moved on to harder things. The ones who didn't became examples.

Fear gripped me as I suddenly and viscerally realized I was the example. My stomach dropped, dread coursing through me.

She rushed out. "Don't back down. If he touches you, grab something…a brick, stick, anything."

She stepped to the fence.

She shouted at Antonio's gang, "Any of you try me and see what happens."

Antonio's crew shifted, circling but watching her carefully. My mother stood there like a lioness guarding her cub. Sweat burned down my spine. My heart hammered, smothering their jeers. Fear twisted with pride inside me.

Antonio stepped into the street. So, did I.

We circled each other slowly, like boxers testing distance. The crowd widened. Waiting.

I decided to throw the first punch but missed his face by an inch. I stumbled from the momentum. He drove punch after punch into my ribcage. I gasped in pain, trying to shield myself, but he was stronger.

Desperate, I bit his side, anything to make him loosen

his grip. His arm locked around my neck tighter.

The world narrowed. Breath thinned.

"Don't you give up! Fight!" my mother's voice cut through the ringing in my ears.

Antonio's grip was squeezing the breath from me, the chorus of shouting, my mother's words echoing like a distant drum. With the last of my strength, I drove my knee upward.

He doubled over.

We both hit the pavement.

Antonio faltered, and his crew surged forward, ready to end it. Older neighbors stepped in, pushing them back and breaking the circle.

I struggled to stand. Each breath burned. My head throbbed where I'd been hit.

***

Then, just as suddenly as it began, the fight ended.

The chaos gave way to silence.

The crowd began to scatter, leaving behind only raw bruises, my trembling hands, and a mingled sense of fear and strange pride. The street felt different.

And then I felt hands under my arm… *Music Man.*

Up close, the scent of liquor clung to him. But his grip was steady. He helped lift me from the pavement as if I weighed nothing.

"I'll take it from here," my mother said, stepping forward.

She pulled me from his arms and wrapped one arm around my waist, holding me upright as we limped back toward the house.

Behind us, the street slowly returned to its rhythm. But something had shifted.

I had stepped into the street.

And the street answered back.

Chapter 3

Opened Wound

I winced as my mother examined my ribs, her careful fingers finding tender spots.

"Ouch!" I exclaimed.

She paused, seeing my eyes squeeze shut against the tears.

"You handled those boys real *good*," she said, her voice both proud and tired. "Ain't no shame in standing tall, you hear me? The world doesn't give you anything if you don't show 'em you got a backbone."

Mother rinsed a washcloth, wrung it out, then placed her hand over mine, showing me how much pressure to use as I cleaned the scrapes on my elbows and knees.

She searched the medicine cabinet for the last few Band-Aids and pressed them gently into place.

"All done," Mother said proudly.

I stood there, wrapped in cotton and adhesive, looking like a walking first-aid kit.

She smiled, memorizing proof I was still standing. "Wash your hands and get ready for dinner."

"What are we having?" I asked, hopeful.

"Black-eyed peas and Jiffy cornbread."

"Again?"

The word slipped out before I could stop it.

Once at the table, I mashed the peas into a paste with the spoon, trying to make them disappear faster.

"Are you complaining?" she asked, one eyebrow raised.

"I could send you to bed on an empty stomach. Do you know how many children would trade places with you in a heartbeat?"

"Yes, ma'am," I muttered.

"I know we've been eating leftovers for the last few days," she added, her tone softening. "My paycheck should come any day now. We just have to hold tight until then."

"Okay," I said, pretending the peas were smothered steak, drenched in A1 sauce, and the cornbread thick and buttery instead of dry around the edges.

"Mom, where's your food? Aren't you hungry?"

"Don't worry about me," she replied. "Eat. I'm alright."

There was no plate, no fork, no spoon in front of her. The smile she offered was steady, but a shadow lurked behind it, something silent and determined.

Her face was calm. Her stomach was not.

I took another bite. Each swallow made the room feel quieter.

When I realized I was the only one eating, I stopped. I set my spoon down and slid the half-finished bowl away.

Chapter 4

Sunday Morning

My mother sat on the edge of my bed and pulled the blanket back before I could hide under it.

"Good morning, sleepyhead. It's time to get up."

"I'm tired, Ma," I groaned.

"You need to get up. We're doing something different this morning. If anybody deserves to stay in bed, it's me." Her voice carried more than insistence. It carried weariness.

"What could be better than going to Ralph's house to play Punch-Out!! on his Nintendo?" I asked.

"Church."

"Oh, no."

"No shoulder shrugging," she said. "Brush your teeth. Wash your face. There will be no negotiations today."

I thought about Ralph, my best friend, the rich kid of the hood in my eyes. His house had new toys at Christmas. An Atari. Later, a Nintendo. His parents laughed together in the kitchen. His father drove trucks. His mother worked at a dealership. They seemed steady.

Our life was different.

I wore my favorite blue-and-red striped polo and tan cargo pants. She wore a bright yellow dress and cork sandals, looking regal as she stepped out of her work clothes.

We walked half a mile to a small storefront church. The brick was chipped. The iron gate rusted. But the doors were open.

Before we even stepped inside, we heard tambourines. Clapping. Feet stomping. Voices rising.

The sanctuary was crowded. We found seats in the back on a creaky wooden bench.

The preacher spoke with fire, telling the story of the woman with the issue of blood, how she reached, how she believed, how she was made whole.

My mother began to cry. Not loud. Just quiet tears sliding down her face.

When the preacher gave the invitation for prayer, a woman turned toward us. She was older, with soft eyes and a firm voice.

She placed a hand on my mother's shoulder and began to pray.

She spoke of burdens. Of exhaustion. Of wounds carried in silence.

My mother broke.

And for the first time, I realized how much she had been holding. I didn't understand everything that was said, but I understood this:

We were not invisible.

As the congregation sang "I Surrender All," my mother pulled me close. The woman wrapped her arms around us both.

It felt like shelter.

Outside, the heat greeted us again.

"What is your name, dear?" the woman asked. "My name is Ella. This is my son, Jacob."

"I'm Mrs. Candors. My husband is one of the deacons here."

She looked at my mother.

"When I hugged you in there, I felt like that was the Lord telling you to come home."

Then she turned to me.

"Young man, God has His hand on your life. You hold on to Him, hear me?"

"Yes, ma'am."

Her words settled somewhere deep inside me.

"Where is his father?" she asked gently.

My mother's voice stayed steady. "He left me before my son was born. I haven't heard from him since."

Mrs. Candors squeezed her hand. "You're not alone anymore," she said. Then she smiled. "I made fried catfish, collard greens, yams, cornbread… and chocolate cake. Y'all come eat with us."

My stomach answered before my mouth could.

Behind the church sat a brown Chevrolet Caprice station wagon.

Deacon Candors joined us, shaking hands firmly.

I jumped toward the car. A gentle hand stopped me.

"Son," he said, smiling, "a gentleman lets the lady get in first."

I stepped back.

My mother entered the car.

And for the first time, I felt like we were ushered into something new.

Chapter 5

The Quiet Years

There is a difference between being alone and building a life. For a long time, I convinced myself I was thriving. People depended on me, and I always showed up. The boy who once felt unstable had grown into a man others leaned on. Order replaced chaos, and discipline replaced impulse.

From the outside, my life appeared complete. The evenings told a different story. After the meetings ended and the sanctuary lights dimmed, I often lingered, not because I had more to do, but because there was nowhere pressing to return to.

My home was kept neat, quiet, and predictable.

I convinced myself that peace was supposed to feel this way. Yet, it didn't always.

Loneliness is subtle. It hides within achievement and camouflages itself as purpose. I learned how to lead, guide, and counsel, but what I had not yet learned was how to share space without guarding it.

I noticed small things: couples lingering in the parking lot after church, fathers carrying sleeping children to their cars, and women laughing in ways that suggested their joy would be heard again at home.

I was not bitter, but I was aware.

I buried myself in responsibility, convinced that productivity could substitute for partnership.

It worked… until it didn't.

Success fills a room, but it does not warm it. Some nights, I would sit in the quiet and confront a question I had long avoided:

Was I protecting my peace or avoiding vulnerability?

There is a key difference between the two. One preserves strength, the other preserves fear.

I had seen the devastation and instability that it could bring to a household and had lived through its consequences. Part of me believed that restraint was a sign of maturity, thinking that by maintaining distance, I could avoid repeating the patterns of the past.

But distance carries its own cost.

A man can master discipline yet still lack intimacy. He can preach commitment without ever being tested by it. For the first time, I understood that a calling does not excuse you from accountability; in fact, it deepens it.

If I were ever to love again, it would require more than simply being ready. It would require honesty, patience, and the willingness to be known without the need for performance. Somewhere in those quiet years, something shifted.

Not desperation.

Not urgency.

Clarity.

I stopped asking whether companionship would disrupt my life and began to consider whether it might refine it.

I stopped assuming that solitude was a sign of strength and allowed myself to admit that partnership was not a weakness. I didn't know when it would happen, but I knew I was no longer hiding from the possibility. When a man stops hiding, he begins to see things differently. *That was the season just before everything changed.*

Chapter 6

"Have enough courage to trust love one more time and always one more time." - Maya Angelou

The Appointment

Some Sundays linger, not because of what was said, but because of what quietly began.

I first noticed Lisa Williams beneath the violet-and-gold glow of the sanctuary. Mother Naomi Johnson clasped her hands as if she sensed what neither of us could say.

I was a minister in a black suit, trying not to let faith become routine. Lisa, a composed visitor, followed rules shaped by loss. There was carefulness in how she moved, the kind you only learn after having to start over. Shadows lingered behind her calm expression, traces of mourning or a disappointment she had quietly carried from another place, another time.

We exchanged polite words. Humor eased uncertainty. Something passed, not romance or promise, but recognition.

Lisa felt it too, though she resisted. She had vowed not to trust her heart. She didn't know how long I had prayed for someone honest, not perfect. What happened that morning moved quietly.

I wasn't searching.

Then I saw her, and a mixture of surprise and hope stopped me. I felt strangely exposed, as if I'd been waiting for this moment without realizing it.

She stood near the aisle, slightly apart, deciding if she belonged. Composed, professional, still. Something in my chest settled: not urgency, but recognition.

After the service, Mother Johnson reached her first. I watched as she took Lisa's hand and smiled with knowing warmth. When she motioned for me to join them, I hesitated, then stepped forward.

Conversation came easily, about church, life, nothing needing defense. I joked badly. Lisa teased gently. I noticed her lack of a ring, her disciplined posture. When she assumed I had a wife and children, I waited before correcting her.

"The only family I have is my church family," I said eventually. "And relatives who call when the lights are about to get shut off."

She laughed. It loosened something in both of us, a soft release of tension, the warmth of real connection pushing aside old defenses just for a moment.

When Pastor Moore greeted me as Minister Foster, the moment shifted.

I clarified, "Titles don't matter to me; how one lives does." She listened, measuring sincerity.

As she prepared to leave, instinct told me to retreat.

Instead, I asked, "May I walk you to your car?"

We talked slowly about work, rest, and life. At the door, I spoke honestly.

"I'd like to see you again."

"We'll see what happens," she replied.

Honest.

Open.

I hugged her longer than I intended. My heart pounded, a quiet longing, mixed with fear that I might be moving too fast, and I felt her hesitation soften just before we let go.

That afternoon, I prayed differently, not for answers, but for clarity.

***

In the weeks that followed, Lisa returned. We exchanged numbers. Conversations deepened. Saturdays became shared, walking through crowded malls, laughing, discovering each other without pretense. One afternoon, caught in a sudden downpour, we took cover beneath a bakery awning.

Rain blurred the world around us.

Lisa surprised me by singing a few lines from an old Al Green song, her voice low, a smile hidden at the edge of her mouth.

I joined in, off-key.

We laughed, and something unguarded settled between us in the hush of the rain.

***

Two months in, we committed.

When I asked her to marry me, joy came easily. Fear followed quietly.

Then came the news, unexpected, life-altering.

Lisa was *pregnant*.

Joy and fear collided. Love demanded courage. Judgment surfaced in the church. The news spread quietly at first, then with sharper whispers and glances on Sunday mornings.

Some members distanced themselves, offering practiced smiles but avoiding conversation. Others simply stopped coming, and in the prayer circle, one woman squeezed my hand harder than usual, as if to express both worry and support. I learned which pews held condemnation, which ones offered silent prayers for us, even if words were never spoken. I carried the weight, knowing my position required accountability. Stepping down was painful but necessary.

Through it all, Lisa remained steady, her quiet strength soothing my turmoil and anchoring us both as we faced the uncertainty ahead.

We postponed the wedding.

The Justice of the Peace felt right for now.

***

When we learned we were having a son, we named him Zion, meaning *the dwelling place of God.*

Even as we adjusted to new routines and carried the weight of uncertainty, we found ourselves looking ahead, dreaming of building a home filled with laughter, faith, and second chances. We promised each other that when the time was right, we would celebrate our marriage with loved ones and share our story openly.

For now, our hope was simple: to raise our son in a home guided by love, patience, and the belief that our best days were still to come.

Together, we chose unity.

One household.

One purpose.

The wedding could wait.

Love had already arrived.

Chapter 7

Living Nightmare

The call came at 3:00 a.m.

I was in Houston for an Educational Leadership Conference, asleep in a hotel bed that still smelled like detergent and unfamiliarity, when my phone vibrated against the nightstand.

For a split second, I thought it was an alarm or worse, a mistake. Then I heard Lisa's voice.

Panicked.

Thin.

Fractured.

"Jacob, I'm worried. I'm bleeding," she said. "And it

won't stop."

In an instant, the room disappeared. Just months earlier, we had chosen names, painted the nursery, and folded tiny clothes with care.

Life had felt steady, promising.

"Okay," I said, forcing calm into my voice. "Tell me what happened."

"I woke up to use the bathroom… then it started," Lisa said, communicating through tidal waves of agony. "I'm in pain."

The helplessness was suffocating. I was hundreds of miles away, suspended between responsibility and terror, trying to anchor her while my own fear threatened to take over. We both realize that from where I was, there was little to nothing I could do.

"Have you called 911?" I asked. "Or tried to call India to take you to the hospital?"

"I don't want an ambulance, you know, they freak me out," she said. "India's out of town. So, I will have to drive. I think I can make it if I leave now while the pain is bearable," she whispered, groaning as we spoke. Then her voice broke.

"Just get here if you can leave."

That plea shattered something inside me.

"I'm leaving now," I said. "Nothing is going to happen. I promise." I didn't wait for goodbye.

The Drive

I threw clothes into a bag, barely aware of my hands shaking. Still in pajamas, I ran from the hotel room, keys biting into my palm as I slammed the car door and pulled onto the interstate. Streetlights blurred. Prayers spilled from my mouth, some formed, others raw and desperate.

I checked in with her at every red light.

Every mile felt too slow.

Every second, too long.

When she told me she'd reached the hospital, I exhaled for the first time, but fear stayed seated beside me the entire drive.

The Hospital

I burst through the sliding doors like a man gasping for air.

"My name is Jacob Foster," I said at the desk, breathless. "I'm looking for my wife."

The receptionist typed slowly, *too* slowly, each keystroke a test of restraint.

"She's been moved to the obstetrics floor," she said finally. "Fourth floor. Make a right."

The elevator ride felt endless. When the doors opened, doubt froze me, left or right? I followed instinct, weaving through the sterile maze until I found Room 412.

"Is everything okay with Lisa?" I asked the nurse.

"Sir, who are you?"

"I'm her husband."

"She's sedated," she said gently. "She went into premature labor. The bleeding was caused by placenta previa. The doctor recommends an emergency C-section."

The words hit like a physical blow.

"When?" I asked.

"As soon as the obstetrician arrives."

I didn't wait for more.

Between Fear and Faith

Lisa lay still, pale beneath fluorescent lights, wires threading her body like silent threats. I kissed her forehead, pressed my face to her hair, willing warmth into her skin.

Her eyes fluttered open.

"I'm here," I whispered.

Her fingers found mine. We held on, as if time might steal her away if we let go. I prayed, not eloquently, not confidently, but honestly.

For protection.

For mercy.

For our son.

Moments later, they rolled her toward the operating room. I walked beside her until I couldn't anymore.

Zion

The surgery blurred into sterile sounds and muffled urgency. I stood where they told me, peering over the sheet when I could, heart hammering.

Then…a cry.

Small.

Fragile.

Alive.

Relief collapsed through me like rain after drought.

"He's here," I whispered, tears rising before I could stop them.

Lisa stirred. "Is he okay?"

"He's beautiful," I said. "Five pounds, eight ounces."

The nurse lifted him just enough for her to see. With the last of her strength, Lisa kissed his cheek before drifting back into sleep.

We named him *Zion*, the dwelling place of God.

And in that moment, God felt very close.

Becoming

The days in the NICU were both challenging and unpredictable. The monitors beeped constantly, and the waiting felt like an eternity.

Hours spent at the hospital turned into long nights. I looked at our son in awe, overwhelmed by gratitude but also a sense of unworthiness.

I attended meetings with doctors as they gave updates. Unfamiliar with most of the medical terminology they were using, I scribbled what I could remember in a notebook to brief Lisa on Zion's progress as she recovered.

Restless. A fatherless son entrusted with a son of his own. I did not think to factor any "what-ifs" in this part of my life. Future vague, I was forced to live day by day with God, to help me know what to do every second.

Lisa worked from home, balancing recovery and motherhood. I cooked, cleaned, adjusted schedules, and did whatever it took to hold our small world together. It wasn't easy. But we were not alone.
Ralph and India showed up.
Quietly.
Faithfully.

Exactly when we needed them.

And somewhere between exhaustion and prayer, fear and gratitude, I realized I wasn't just surviving anymore.

33

Chapter 8

True Friends Indeed

R alph and India entered our lives at a time when Lisa and I were no longer exploring the possibilities but were quietly learning the discipline of commitment.

I had known Ralph for more than twenty-five years. I watched him grow from an ambitious, slightly awkward teenager into a man whose presence required no announcement.

Ralph

At thirty-seven, he co-owned multiple IT and web design firms. He was self-made, self-disciplined, and steady. Success came naturally to him, but relationships did not.

Ralph did not rely on charm; he valued substance, honesty, loyalty, and equality. Many admired him, but few could stand beside him—those who could find a man deeply loyal, quietly generous, and unwavering once committed. When Lisa entered my life, Ralph did not demand assurance; he observed.

India

India, on the other hand, assessed the situation. A celebrated radio personality and Lisa's closest friend since college, India carried her instincts like a finely tuned instrument.

With her shoulder-length sister-locks and authenticity shaped by New York, she missed nothing. Her loyalty to Lisa was quiet but immovable. She had seen Lisa survive heartbreak, particularly with Daniel.

One evening, while entertaining radio executives, India spotted him across the room, comfortable beside his wife and young daughter. Without hesitation, she captured the stark reality in a single photograph. There are moments when denial ends.

Grief and Trust

Lisa's grief ran deep, but India kept it in check, and by the time I met Lisa, India's vigilance had matured. She studied me carefully, and I didn't blame her. I shared my story plainly, no pretense, no inflated promises, just the truth of who I was and who I was still becoming.

Trust didn't arrive overnight, but it did arrive. And when it did, India noticed.

True Friendship

Ralph and India would later stand with us through trials that tested more than just our romance. When Lisa's pregnancy came unexpectedly, they did not pull away; they leaned closer.

When whispers circulated and opinions formed, India quietly said, "You didn't fail God. You disappointed people. That's not the same thing." I knew she meant to protect us, not to rebel.

During the emergency C-section that left our baby, Zion, fighting in the neonatal ICU, Ralph and India took shifts at the hospital so we would never sit alone in that waiting room. When we were finally discharged, exhausted and overwhelmed, Ralph lifted the baby bag from my hand

and placed it by the door without asking. No one thanked him; no one needed to.

There are friendships built on convenience, but there are also those forged in fluorescent hospital lighting, held together by an unspoken understanding. Ralph and India were not just friends; they were witnesses. And a covenant feels stronger when witnessed.

Chapter 9

Milestones of Life

Zion's tenth birthday was carefully planned. We wanted it to feel more than just a party; after the fragile beginnings of his life, every milestone felt genuinely earned.

***

The backyard was filled with balloons and streamers.

Zion, dressed as Iron Man, ran across the grass with a carefree joy that only children possess. The other boys, also in superhero costumes, followed him, their capes flying behind them. Ralph and I joined in a game of football, fully aware that our recovery time would be longer than the celebration itself. "I got him! I got him!" Zion shouted after tackling me to the ground.

"You got me, champ," I laughed, brushing grass from my shirt as the other fathers drifted toward the grill in surrender.

Lisa watched from the patio, smiling, not just at the game but at the life unfolding in front of her.

When it came time for cake, India's voice led the chorus, singing louder than anyone else, while Ralph tried to restore order among the impatient hands reaching for frosting. The day moved quickly, filled with laughter, food, and gratitude.

After the guests left and the yard quieted, we gathered inside around the opened gifts. Zion sat cross-legged on the floor, his eyes bright with anticipation.

Lisa and I exchanged a look.

It was time.

I slipped upstairs and returned with three envelopes.

Ralph lifted his fist.

"You know you don't have to pay us for friendship," he teased.

Lisa smiled. "This isn't payment."

Inside each envelope were handwritten letters.

"Ralph," I said, steadying my voice, "I would be honored if you would stand as my best man."

He didn't hesitate. "Of course."

Lisa turned to India. "You already know. But formally, will you be my maid of honor?"

India blinked once, then twice. "You already know the answer."

Finally, I knelt beside Zion, giving a heavy sigh from the excitement of the day.

"Son," I said softly, "would you walk your mother down the aisle?"

He looked up at us, stunned and proud all at once. "In place of Grandpa?"

"Yes."

"Anything for you and Mom!"

He wrapped his arms around us, and in that embrace, I felt something steady, something healed.

***

Later that evening, after Ralph and India had gone home, with pizza boxes stacked and blankets spread across the living room floor, Zion leaned against us with curiosity in his eyes and asked a question.

"Dad, if you're already married, why are you getting married *again*?"

"We're not getting married again," I told him. "We're

renewing our vows. I promised your mother that one day we would celebrate properly, and what will make it perfect is that you'll be part of it."

He nodded, satisfied.

But I wasn't, because I knew what this moment meant to me in a way he could not yet understand. I never walked my mother down an aisle. I never watched my father stand and choose us publicly.

I never saw a covenant honored before witnesses.

My father chose another life, another family, another beginning.

I carried that absence quietly for years.

And as I watched Zion drift to sleep, secure beneath our roof, I decided long before the ceremony would begin that he would never wonder if he had been chosen. He would never question where he stood. The void I inherited would end with me.

Chapter 10

Saturday Morning

The sunrise streaming through the living area's windows was a familiar sight that brought a refreshing feeling, perfect for a nice cup of coffee. The sounds of fishing boats and our sprinkler system filled our Lakeview dream home.

Though my neck was a little sore from sleeping upright with Lisa neatly snuggled under my arm, I gently laid her head on the nearest pillow and headed to the kitchen to prepare a small breakfast for Lisa and Zion.

Moving through the kitchen, I let the morning's warmth settle over me. Starting our mornings together, just the three of us, safe and happy under one roof, grounded me.

I had only dreamed of this contentment years ago, and I still sometimes couldn't believe it was real.

The clank of pans and the pop of a toaster woke Lisa to a tempting aroma. She yawned and stretched.

"That smells delicious, babe," she said, peering sleepily over the couch. Her untamed hair was a comical scene, usually kept under a bonnet. Without it, she looked like Thing 1 and Thing 2 from Dr. Seuss, but to me, she was *adorable*. I laughed quietly.

"My hair is messed up, isn't it?" Lisa guessed, catching my expression before I could answer.

"Babe, you look fine." I grinned. "It's amazing how the businesswoman I met ten years ago is just as beautiful with messy hair and drool."

"I was drooling?" Lisa feigned shock, eyes wide.

"This isn't new. You've always drooled," I said, grinning.

"So, who's the one who snores and passes gas in his sleep?" Lisa shot back, flashing a playful grin.

"Mom and Dad, you're disturbing my sleep," Zion groaned, pulling his pillow over his head.

"It's time to get up anyway, little man. Don't you want to eat breakfast?" I called over the countertop at the pile of blankets that always seemed endless to put away.

"Yes, but after I wake up," Zion muttered. "If I didn't know better, I'd think he worked full-time," I said to Lisa.

"He is definitely his *father's* son," Lisa quipped.

"I can't argue with you there," I conceded.

Zion stood up, mummified in his blankets, looking around as if he'd just seen the aftermath of a tornado.

"Yep, we're going to have *you* pick this all up, young man," Lisa instructed in a motherly tone.

"But *Mom*, there's so much to pick up. What about my birthday?" Zion protested.

"That was *yesterday*, today's a new day. A little work won't hurt you, son," I said, setting plates at the breakfast nook.

"But isn't the housekeeper coming? She can clean this up, right?" Zion bargained, trying to negotiate, as he always does.

"Son, you heard your mother," I said sternly.

"Let him eat first, then clean up, and please lower your voice. It's too early, Honey." Lisa pleaded. "Don't worry, baby; Mommy will help you."

As I sat for breakfast, Lisa spread grape jelly on her bagel. Zion, next to me, seemed proud and relieved he'd won his mother's sympathy as we ate.

I let it go, choosing my battles.

Though I had to take a deep breath, loosening any

unnoticed tension. Lisa sensed it.

"What's on your agenda today?" Lisa asked, intentionally shifting my thoughts from their deep focus.

"I'm meeting Ralph for a workout, then basketball. After, I'll take Zion to the barber and hang out. When's your appointment? Isn't it usually now?" I glanced at my watch.

"Oh no! It's 8:30 this *morning*! What time is it now?"

"Babe, it's almost *9:00!*"

"I need to call the beauty salon to see if my hairstylist can squeeze me in."

Lisa called *Unique Stylz. Sheila, her stylist, rescheduled her for two o'clock* after a canceled appointment. She showered and dressed upstairs.

Zion and I cleaned the living area, though I finished alone. I was as particular about organization as Lisa.

With the last dish loaded and counters wiped, I set the towel down, satisfied. Upstairs, I changed and kissed Lisa goodbye.

Zion, engrossed in his game, mumbled, "Bye, Dad," without looking up.

***

I spotted Ralph at the gym door.

After we checked in, we noticed the weight area was packed, except for the squat machine, so we headed there.

Pressing the weight off the bar, Ralph grunted with every

fiber of his being for seven reps until his knees began to tremble. I stood nearby, ready to spot him if needed. When Ralph let out a loud grunt and set the weight back in place, the iron plates echoed off the walls.

"Ralph, you only had three reps left. What happened?"

"Man, you must be *crazy* if you think I was going to do *that* many reps! Go ahead and take off those 45s and put on one of the 10s lying beside you," Ralph demanded.

"Stop being so pushy, man! I've got this!" I said jokingly.

"Ralph, you were talking big when you started," I reminded. Beads of sweat formed on Ralph's brow.

"Come on, give me three more!" I switched to trainer mode.

"I'm not the one who was a football player. I'm a businessman, it's all about the Benjamins; that's *my* specialty."

"Are you finished? Because I need to get my sets in before we play ball, and I can't stay too long since I need to leave so my wife won't miss her hair appointment," Ralph said, wiping his face with a towel he'd left at the counter. Then he walked away, leaving me to finish my reps alone.

After finishing my reps, I met Ralph at the front desk, where he tossed a towel at me, aiming at chest level.

"Sightseeing," he replied, nodding toward two women in yoga gear who checked us out as they walked by.

One of them winked at me, undressing me with her eyes.

"He's married," Ralph said, defending me.

Then, turning to the women as they passed, Ralph called out, "But I'm available."

As we headed toward the basketball court, I urged, "Man, we need to get going. I'm already on a tight schedule."

"So, how are things going with you and the business?" I asked as we approached the doorway.

"Everything is going well. We just closed another huge contract for cybersecurity with an investment firm."

"Wow! That's great! What's the count now, about seven contracts since we last spoke?" I prompted.

"No, man, we're almost at nine contracts, and we're in negotiations to secure our tenth one within the next month."

"Brother, it sounds like your business is doing *extremely* well," I congratulated, giving Ralph a fist bump.

"But I'm not going to lie, man; when I first started this tech company, I had no idea it would grow to where it is now."

As we moved to the empty side of the court, exchanging free throws and layups, I asked, "So now that everything's going well business-wise, what's up with your love life?" We warmed up together until it was our turn to join the three-on-three game at the other end.

"It is what it is. It's not that I don't believe in love; I'm just too busy."

"I totally feel you on that. It was like that for me, too, before I met Lisa, if you remember." I bounced the ball once before taking a jump shot.

Ralph recovered the ball before he continued. "Life has unfortunately given me a hint that a relationship may not be for me after all. Someday, but I don't see it happening now. Dating is so unpredictable nowadays anyway." He bounced the ball at the free-throw line before making the shot.

"Would you say your past relationships have made you hesitant to open yourself up to the possibility of love again?" I asked.

"Maybe, I guess we will have to see."

"I am sure there is someone out there for you."

"Don't get me wrong; I do want to get married one day. I just haven't found the right person yet. I'm looking for a woman with as much drive as I have. She should know where she's going. I want someone I can talk with, nothing too deep, like a friend, but one I'm attracted to. And for kids, I'd like one or two so we can grow as a family through life. Is that too much to ask?" Ralph tossed me the ball so I could practice my jump shot.

"I don't think that's asking too much. But I thought you were the kind of guy who liked a high-profile life. Am I wrong?"

"That's the thing. I thought at first that was the lifestyle I wanted, but as I got older and had a moment of reflection, that kind of life felt short-lived for me," Ralph shared, his voice carrying the weight of his past experiences.

I considered mentioning India as a worthwhile pursuit, but I decided to keep that thought to myself, feeling uncertain if it was the right time, especially given the recent events with Ashley. I was curious about what happened to Ashley, a woman he met on Instagram, since they were doing well before she vanished.

"What happened to Ashley?" I inquired about the woman he met on a dating site. From my impression, things seemed to be going well with her on the surface.

"Once she saw my house and expensive cars, she saw an opportunity, and dollar signs. She invited strangers to my house on the weekends. She planned wild parties I didn't want. She even drove my new Range Rover over the curb, denting the rim. I let her take it to the mall. She laughed it off in the most annoying, squeaky voice, thinking everything was okay. I had to tell her that her hourglass figure couldn't pay for the damage. I was stressed, to say the least. When New Edition said, '*You can't trust a big butt and a smile*,' I should have believed them. Man, we were like night and day. She had the *body* but not the *brain*."

Ralph's response reminded me of the comparison India made about Jerome last night. I hadn't realized how similar their situations were until that moment.

"It seems like you and India need someone who shares similar values, work ethics, understanding, and support. You never know how God will reveal that the person you least expect could be right in front of you," I said as he nodded in agreement.

After the three-on-three match, we retired our shoelaces to prep for a full-court pickup game. This time, Ralph and I joined opposing teams, ready to play to fifteen points.

The sounds of bouncing basketballs, foul calls, and squeaking sneakers echoed across the court as we sprinted back and forth until his team emerged victorious.

Chapter 11

A Matter of Time

I was running late not only for Lisa's appointment but also for Zion's haircut. Although I had calculated the time to leave the gym and was only a few minutes off, I hadn't considered the traffic caused by a semi-truck that had jackknifed in the middle of the lane. This accident forced a significant detour onto the side roads running parallel to the highway.

Feeling the weight of knowing that Lisa had already missed her first appointment, I couldn't bear the thought of being the reason she would miss her follow-up appointment, too.

The situation was even more stressful because it was a Saturday, and there were no other appointments available. I had to get there no matter what the cost.

I navigated the frontage road, struggling to keep up with traffic, and found myself in a series of desperate prayers. Each traffic light conspired against me, turning red as I approached. I was 15 to 20 minutes behind schedule when I arrived home.

As I came to a screeching halt in our curved driveway and approached the front door, Lisa rushed past me and headed straight for her car without saying a word. There was little time for me to explain myself, and I could sense her frustration as she tossed her handbag onto the passenger seat, put on her sunglasses, and closed the car door firmly. She was growing weary of my excuses for being late for events that were important to her. Even though I tried to justify my punctuality at work and at Zion's games, Lisa felt that I didn't prioritize her. Looking at the evidence she presented, it became clear that her feelings were valid, despite my intentions.

I walked into the house, feeling queasy and unsure about how to fix things. To make matters worse, Zion sat on the couch, shaking his head at me as if I had just come back from the principal's office, which I understood all too well as a principal myself with kids who often got into trouble. Now I am getting a taste of my own medicine. "Mom's upset, huh?" I asked, trying to assess how bad the situation was.

"*Dad*, let's say I stayed quiet while Mom walked around the house talking to herself about you under her breath. Dad, the things she was saying were too harsh for my virgin ears."

"That bad, huh?"

"Yep." He replied.

"Dad."

"Yeah, son?"

"I want you to know that if you don't make it through the night because of Mom, I will always have a place for you in my heart." Zion stood up and placed his hand on my shoulder, as if sharing his final sentiments.

"Boy, that's *messed* up! You are wrong for that one, Zion. But you got me!" I chuckled. "Let's get to the barbershop to get your haircut before your mother comes home. I want to get *one* thing at least right today." I joked as we left the house for the barbershop.

Mr. Dorsey's Barbershop

The scent of barbershop alcohol filled the air, tickling our noses as we entered the barbershop's threshold. The humming of clippers, faint conversations, and as a customer with a fresh haircut passed by, proudly patting his newly styled hair. An old, rusty bell hung over the door, ringing softly to greet those who entered and bid farewell to those who left.

Dorsey's Barbershop has been a historical landmark and family-owned business since 1955, deeply rooted in the community's cultural tapestry. More than a place for haircuts, Dorsey's has served as a social hub and a second home for many. Generations of patrons have gathered here to exchange ideas, share stories, and build connections, reinforcing the barbershop as a cornerstone of community life. The leather and strop used for honing straight-edge razor blades adorn the sides of every barber's chair, as in the days of old, giving the barbershop a nostalgic feel, as if you had entered a time capsule to the late 1950s.

A squeaky ceiling fan slowly spun above, struggling to provide relief to customers. A group of men of all ages sat, entertaining themselves with politics, sports, and religion as they waited for their turn for a haircut. The walls, adorned with posters featuring hairstyles from stylish fades to afros, provided a lovely backdrop for the urban country club.

Hanging on the wall in old picture frames were photographs of Mr. Dorsey in his younger years, alongside musical greats, local and state politicians, and the who's who of national celebrities. On the counter, he kept wooden boxes filled with 3x5 cards that detailed the clipper sizes of these individuals, in case they came back into town to see him. The framed autographs displayed on rusty nails around the shop added authenticity to his remarkable stories.

As a young boy at the genesis of his teenage years, I

occasionally found myself getting into trouble. During those times, my mother would often take me to the barbershop, not just for a haircut but also to be around additional positive male influences. They would lightly counsel my mother through stories of wisdom from those who had raised their own sons with similar challenges. It was a community where families took care of one another, even correcting one another.

My mother knew that this barbershop also represented tough love from male figures if I needed it. One pivotal moment stands out: Mr. Dorsey, noticing my defiant attitude, spoke of his younger days, of facing challenges much like mine, and of how perseverance and humility led him to success, giving my mother hope not to give up on the man I would one day become.

"How are you doing, Mr. Dorsey?" I asked as Zion, and I settled into two rusty red pleather chairs positioned in front of Mr. Dorsey's barber chair. The worn upholstery served as a testament to years of use.

"Well, well, well! Jacob, it's so good to see you, son. Where have you been all this time?" Mr. Dorsey replied excitedly, pausing his work on a client's beard.

"I went away to college," I began. "After graduating, I worked as a schoolteacher before going back for my master's degree. And I am a principal now."

"You don't say. I guess coming to the barbershop when

you were younger finally knocked some sense into that hard head of yours." Mr. Dorsey said, jokingly, with a chuckle.

"And I am a minister too at my church," I said, knowing he would be amazed. "You don't say!" he exclaimed, shocked. "God works in mysterious ways, but I always knew you had it in you. Sometimes, a mother's prayer and the love of others can turn a life around. But times have changed. Kids today don't listen. The barbershop has lost its old influence, but I do my best to hold on to it. There was a time when this place was meant for men and boys to learn, laugh, and grow together. Not anymore. Young barbers care more about money than their impact on the community." Mr. Dorsey continued shaving as the client lay still, half-shaved and almost asleep in the chair over the sink.

"Trust me, I see it every day. You wouldn't believe the stories I could tell you if I had the time," I said, feeling a nudge against my arm as Zion hinted at wanting to be acknowledged. "Oh, there's one more… I mean, two more special updates," I added.

"I'm assuming one of them is the young man you brought in with you?" Mr. Dorsey inquired.

"Yes, sir," I replied humbly.

"What's your name, young man?" Mr. Dorsey smiled at him.

"My name is Zion," he answered.

"Zion That is a wonderful name," Mr. Dorsey replied. "I have an interesting story to tell you. I bet you didn't know that I cut your father's hair when he was your age."

"Really!" Zion sounded amazed. "Dad, you must be *old*," he said, turning towards me.

"I am not that old, son," I replied, feeling a little embarrassed.

"But wasn't that a *long* time ago?" Zion said seriously. "Son, it wasn't that long ago."

Mr. Dorsey chuckled as he finished up his client's beard, letting the chair rise to an upright position.

"Yep. He's your son, alright." Mr. Dorsey said, handing the client a mirror to inspect his finished work.

Handing the client the mirror was always a formality, although Mr. Dorsey knew every client's hair, just as a Championship quarterback knew game plays. Seeing the client was satisfied, Mr. Dorsey brushed away the excess hair before applying aftershave talc. With a swift motion, he snapped off the apron, as quick and professional as a bullfighter, and gave another quick sweep of the seat of the barber's chair in preparation for Zion, who was his next appointment.

"So, what else is new, Jacob?" Mr. Dorsey placed the apron around Zion's shoulders while elevating the barber's chair with the lever located at the base of the chair.

"Well, sir, I am also married to the most beautiful woman

in the world," I said, my chest swelling with pride.

"Is that so? Would you happen to have a picture of this beautiful woman?" he asked, mimicking my statement playfully. I could feel a smile creeping up on my face as I reached for my wallet and pulled out a photo of my wife, Lisa, her bright eyes and warm smile captured.

"*Oooo wee!*" He sounded like a cowboy's howl. "Jacob, she IS beautiful. You've done great for yourself, son." Mr. Dorsey said, endearingly. "I am so proud of how things turned out for you. I can't wait to tell my wife about you when I get home. We have been wondering how you and your mother were doing. If you talk to her anytime soon, please let her know my wife and I said hello, you hear?" he requested warmly.

He took out a new 3x5 card and a pen from his antique barbershop cabinet to write down Zion's haircut measurement.

Amazed at the sight and curious at the same time, I asked, "Mr. Dorsey, would you still happen to have *my* card?" I asked, feeling nostalgic.

"Hmm, let's see," he said, turning to the cabinet to thumb through the drawer to find my name, taking a few seconds to hand me my 3x5 index card with worn ink. "Here you go, *Jacob Foster.*" He sounded my name out, using the spectacles around his neck.

"I can't believe you *still* have my card after all these years!" I exclaimed in amazement as I showed Zion my personalized index card. The card read:

"Hi-top fade, complete with a designer part that starts at the right temple and runs to the back of the head with initials."

"Dad, that sounds *cool!* Can I have that?" Zion asked eagerly.

"That was a long time ago, son. I think you should

settle for a nice low-cut fade for now. Besides, a low fade will make you look like a distinguished gentleman," I replied, hoping to dissuade him.

"*Ahhhh*, Dad," Zion's expression fell as if I had popped his balloon of excitement.

Feeling guilty, I said, "Tell you what. How about you have the designer do the part you want, if it's not *too* long, and I'll have Mr. Dorsey give you a low fade instead of a high one. Does that sound good?"

"Thanks, Dad!" Zion agreed.

Overhearing our conversation, Mr. Dorsey noted the request and began cutting Zion's hair.

I sat back in my chair, phone in hand, scrolling through social media to pass the minutes amid the low hum of chatter in the barbershop. The rusty doorbell chimed, and a familiar figure stepped in, a medium-built man dressed in casual sportswear, hat backward, headphones around his neck, lollipop tucked in the corner of his mouth. He made his way to a chair a seat down from Mr. Dorsey's, setting up his clippers with careful precision… and then it clicked.

"Zeus?" I called, rising from my seat. "It's Jacob!"

His eyes widened, recognition spreading across his face. "Jake! Man, it's been ages. How the hell are you?"

We clasped hands like old teammates, the memory of our high school football days, him on the defensive line, me at safety, flashing between us.

Back then, Zeus had been over 350 pounds; now, he looked lean, strong, almost unrecognizable.

As we caught up, marriage, Zion, my work as a principal, church, Zeus leaned in, lowering his voice enough to pull me with him. His eyes held a quiet intensity that hadn't been there before.

"*Yo…* this might sound wild, but hear me out."

I frowned. "What is it?"

He glanced toward the front of the shop, then back at me. "You know the salon next door? Them ladies been talking."

"Talking about what?"

He hesitated, then shrugged. "Man, you know how it is.

But your name came up."

I said nothing

"Back in the day, around the time you left for college, there was this girl… Tina." He watched my face carefully. "They sayin' she had a daughter."

My stomach dropped.

"And some folks think the kid might be yours." He continued.

I froze. The sound of clippers filled the silence between us, loud and mechanical, like it was cutting through more than hair.

"Wait… what are you talking about?"

"I'm telling you what's been going around," he said, nodding toward the wall we shared with the salon. "She's been coming back lately. Getting her hair done next door. That's why it's picking up again."

My pulse thudded in my ears. "For twenty years? Nobody said anything for twenty years?"

He lifted a shoulder. "You know how people are. Stuff fades… then comes back when somebody shows up again."

The clippers buzzed as he turned to set up his next client, like the conversation was already over.

"I didn't want to leave you blind," he added. "If there's anything to it… you might want to check. DNA test or something." A brief pause. "If it's true, she'd be about twenty now."

The words landed heavily.

Zion shifted in Mr. Dorsey's chair nearby, twisting around to look at me, his eyes wide.

"Dad… do I have a big sister?"

The question hit harder than anything Zeus had said.

I forced a smile that didn't hold. "No, son. I don't think so. This is just… talk."

But even as I said it, doubt crept in, quiet, persistent.

Mr. Dorsey shot Zeus a sharp look. "Hey. Don't be putting that kind of thing on a man if you don't know it's true."

Zeus didn't argue. Just nodded once, subdued now.

"It's just… people been talking more since she came back," he muttered. "Figured you should hear it from me."

The shop suddenly felt different, smaller, heavier. Like the air had thickened.

A rumor *that old* shouldn't still have weight.

But this one did.

I stood, barely aware of what I said as I made my way toward the door. The noise of the shop dulled behind me, like I was stepping out of it and into something else.

Outside, the light hit hard.

I paused on the sidewalk, trying to steady my breathing.

Lisa.

The thought of telling her tightened something deep in my chest. Questions. Doubt. That look in her eyes when something didn't sit right.

I ran through the conversation before it even happened, what I'd say, how I'd explain it, and whether she'd believe me, or if this would change everything.

Behind me, the door opened briefly. I glanced back.

Zeus stood in the doorway, giving a small, solemn nod. Then the door closed, and the bell on the door rang, and the question followed me home.

***

Lisa was still at her hair appointment when we arrived home on that warm Saturday afternoon. The sun was at its peak as we entered the house. The only sound heard was the jingling of the keys as I opened the door.

A few minutes later, like clockwork, my phone buzzed from a text from Lisa that read:

Honey,

If you get back home before me, please follow through on the "Honey-Do-List" you promised, beginning with the laundry. The first load should already be done and ready to fold. The second load of clothes, which are Zion's, is prepared for washing. Have Zion clean his room, especially under his bed.

The landscapers are running a little behind. Please remind them

63

to be extra careful with the edging around my flower bed and rose
garden.

I love you. (hearts emojis)

***

After completing the *to-do list* of my own deep cleaning and taking a much-needed shower, I tried to unwind by watching *ESPN*, hoping the scurrying of thoughts in my head would settle down. However, I couldn't shake the feeling that it was the right time to let Lisa know what I had learned from the barbershop, or to investigate further, rather than cause unnecessary friction over hearsay. I could not go to Lisa, not entirely sure. That would be a disaster waiting to happen.

***

I decided to call Ralph to hear his thoughts and see if he had anything reasonable to say while Zion was upstairs.

"What's up, Jacob!" Ralph answered.

"Hey man, *whatchu* doing?" I asked to gauge whether I would have his undivided attention before I continued.

"Nothing much, man, on my laptop checking how my stocks performed after the market closed, which was not too shabby. But besides that, I'm about to make myself a sandwich and relax. Why?" He replied.

"I got something to run by you real fast, to see what you think," I said, and began explaining the conversation at the

Barbershop with Zeus.

"Wow! Man, that's heavy. People think Tina's daughter is yours?" Ralph asked after I finished speaking.

"You know how rumors are, Ralph. C'mon man! You believe it, too?" I said, taken aback.

"Jacob, I know you've changed and all, living for the Lord and *thangs* like that, but you've got to know, when you were in high school and even college, you weren't exactly a choir boy. You know what I am *sayin*? I'm being straight up with you. You know as well as I do that we are not immune to life's surprises," Ralph said, sounding slightly convinced.

"So, you think it may be true?" I asked worriedly.

"I am not saying it's true or not, but because everyone knew you two were an item for some time, it would be easy to believe the rumor was true. Who else could she have been with? As far as I could see at the time, Tina was only faithful to you." He said somberly.

"What am I going to do, man? Lisa had already been through enough in her life. I also saw something like this with my own mom when I was young. It shook her to the core."

"The past does have a strange way of repeating itself, huh?" Ralph said in reflection.

"Yeah, but in my mom's case, my father ran off with another woman and had kids with her, but in my case, I never knew this child existed."

"How long has it been now, roughly 20 years, since you've seen her, right?" Ralph recollected.

"Yep. You are right. She's a grown woman now." I said.

"Maybe it wouldn't be so bad after all," Ralph said, looking at the brighter side of things.

"But then, I have missed over 20 years of a little girl's life as an absentee father." I sighed. "There is no winning in this situation, man."

"Calm down, calm down. We are getting way ahead of ourselves right now. We still don't know whether this child or a grown woman belongs to you in this case. But let's hope for your sake she's not."

"I think I need to tell Lisa, from how it's beginning to sound. I wouldn't want to be left in the dark if I were in my wife's place." I said in despair.

"Wait, wait, my man," Ralph said in urgency. "I am not looking forward to attending your funeral, because if you tell her NOW, she's going to kill you, bro," Ralph continued, a hint of seriousness beneath his joke. "Tell you what. Let me do some recon on this for you and get back with you in a few days."

"*Bra'*, I may be dead in a few days!" I replied, my voice strained, feeling as if I were already running out of time, the weight of the situation pressing down on me.

"I just thought of a few solid connections I can call who may know how to get in contact with Tina, to get to the bottom of this. Just relax, bro, I got you. 48 hours.” Ralph said with assurance.

“*48 hours* and not a minute more!” I said, feeling as if I had put my neck in the guillotine as we ended the call.

Emotionally and physically exhausted from the day, I decided to take a quick nap before Lisa came home. Before I could close my eyes well enough, Zion came downstairs to check to see how I was doing before he asked for permission to play his game.

“Dad, are you ok?” Zion sounded a little concerned and sensitive to my countenance.

“Listen, son, I am deeply sorry for what happened at the Barbershop this morning,” I said somberly.

“It’s ok, Dad, I mean, it was not like you knew, and besides, I know you wouldn’t have held that kind of news from Mom if you did. I just hope she will understand just as much as I did after you tell her.” Zion’s voice was filled with empathy.

“Thanks, son,” I said with gratitude.

Zion came over to where I reclined to hug me before returning to his room to play his game. I fell asleep soon afterwards.

Chapter 12

Shadows of the Past, Strength of the Present

Lisa called out, "Honey, I'm home!"

Her voice was light, cheerful, like she hadn't seen us in days. The rustle of shopping bags followed her in, filled with clothes for her and Zion, along with beauty and haircare products from the mall. The faint scent of new fabric and perfume drifted into the room.

"I missed you, sweetie," she said, wrapping me in a tight hug and a kiss.

Her presence filled the room, and should have settled me.

It didn't.

I opened my mouth to speak, but the words caught somewhere between my throat and my thoughts.

Before I could try again, she called Zion over, holding up a shirt and belt. "Come here, baby. Try these on. I think you're growing faster than I can keep up."

As she shifted into mom mode, I watched quietly, waiting for the right moment.

It didn't come.

Not yet.

"Your hair looks amazing," I said, forcing a little extra enthusiasm into my voice. "Sheila did a great job."

Lisa smiled and gave a small twirl. "Thank you. It's nice to feel like myself again. Amazing what a little time to yourself can do."

"It reminds me of the first time I saw you at church," I said.

Her cheeks warmed slightly. "Well, maybe I should switch it up every two weeks then, if I'm going to get that kind of reaction."

Zion came rushing back down the stairs, showing off each outfit, spinning while Lisa inspected every detail.

"Perfect," she said. "Turn around, let me see the back. Okay… yeah, we're keeping all of it."

"What do you think?" she asked.

Zion and I both nodded.

"Now," she said, kicking off her sneakers and settling into the chair, "how was your day? You two didn't have too much fun without me, did you?"

Zion didn't answer. He muttered something about putting his clothes away and disappeared upstairs faster than usual.

I watched him go.

"Wow…" I said under my breath.

Lisa frowned slightly. "What's wrong with him? His stomach okay? You didn't feed him anything crazy, did you?"

"No, nothing like that."

She studied me now, her expression shifting. "Is everything okay? You both are acting a little strange."

I grabbed a bottle of water, more for something to do than anything else.

"Yeah… everything's fine."

She didn't buy it.

Her eyes lingered on me a second longer than usual.

I sat down, twisting the bottle cap between my fingers.

"What's got you so fidgety?" she asked.

"This morning started normal," I said. "Gym with Ralph, picked up Zion and took him to the barbershop…"

She reached out, placing her hand lightly on my forearm.

"You're telling me things I already know," she said. "Why are you nervous?"

I took a breath, trying to steady myself.

"Lisa, I…"

Her phone rang.

She glanced at the screen. "I'm sorry, this is my boss. I have to take this."

I nodded, sitting there as she walked away, her voice carrying through the house—focused, sharp, professional.

By the time she returned, something had shifted.

Not in her.

In the moment.

"I've got to get started on something for work," she said quickly, already moving. "We'll talk in a bit, okay?"

"Yeah," I said.

But the moment was gone.

***

When I walked into the bedroom later, Lisa was already propped against the headboard, laptop open, and papers spread across the bed. Her fingers moved quickly across the keys, focused.

"Are you free to talk now?" I asked.

"Not really," she said. Then, after a beat, "But I'd rather deal with it now than think about it all night."

She shifted just enough for me to sit.

I took a breath. "Lisa… I ran into someone at the barbershop today. An old teammate."

She kept her eyes on the screen. "Okay…"

"He mentioned something. About a girl I dated back then. Tina."

Her fingers slowed.

"He said she had a daughter."

Now she looked at me.

"A daughter?"

"Yeah." My mouth felt dry. "And… there's talk she could be mine."

Silence settled between us.

Not empty.

Tight.

"Are you saying this might be true?" she asked.

"I don't know," I said quickly. "I didn't know anything about this until today. I swear."

She held my gaze for a moment.

"For twenty years?" she asked. "No one said anything?"

"No."

She leaned back slightly, exhaling through her nose. One hand came up to her temple, pressing lightly like she was trying to steady something.

"That doesn't make sense," she said.

"I know."

Another pause.

"I needed to tell you," I said. "I didn't want you hearing

it from somewhere else."

I watched her closely.

Lisa didn't react the way most people would.

No raised voice. No sharp questions.

Just… stillness.

Her fingers rested on the edge of her laptop, unmoving, like she had forgotten what she was doing entirely.

"I hear you," she said.

But something in her tone didn't land all the way.

Her eyes drifted, not far, just enough to tell me she wasn't fully in the room anymore.

I had seen that look before.

Not often.

But enough to know…

Lisa wasn't reacting.

She was processing.

And when she got quite like that, it meant something deeper was turning beneath the surface.

"I need to finish this," she said quietly. "We'll talk more later."

"Okay."

I sat there a second longer.

Waiting.

She didn't look back.

That night, the room was quiet, the moonlight stretching across the walls in thin silver lines.

Lisa's hand rested over mine.

Steady.

Familiar.

But something had shifted.

Not broken.

Not gone.

Just… different.

And I couldn't tell yet what that difference would become.

Chapter 13

Sunday Morning

Zion's eyes were wide with worry.

"Dad… Mom's not here."

The words hit harder than they should have.

The house felt too quiet, the kind of quiet that made every thought louder than it needed to be.

"I'm sure she's okay," I said, already moving, checking her phone, calling her name, scanning rooms I knew she wasn't in.

I tried not to read too much into it.

But Lisa didn't just leave.

She *needed* to.

There was a difference.

She hadn't argued, hadn't accused, hadn't shut down.

She had just… stepped away. And somehow, that felt heavier than anything she could've said.

I called India.

"She probably needed space," she said, calm as ever. "You know how she is when something sits heavy on her."

Yeah.

I knew.

Still didn't make it easier.

Zion shifted in his chair, restless. "She didn't say where she was going?"

"No," I said. "But she'll be back."

I hoped that was true.

***

The garage door finally broke the silence. Zion jumped up before I could say anything. Lisa stepped inside a moment later, dressed in workout clothes, her oversized college sweatshirt hanging loose around her as if it were doing more than keeping her warm.

"Hey," I said, moving toward her. "I was getting worried."

She nodded once. "I know."

No hug.

Not right away.

"I just… needed some space," she said. "To think."

"That's fair," I replied carefully.

She set her keys down, slower than usual.

"After everything last night…" she continued, "I didn't want to react the wrong way."

I watched her, trying to read what she wasn't saying.

"I've been through things like this before, Jacob," she added. "Not the same, but close enough."

Her tone stayed even.

Controlled.

"Secrets… they land differently."

"I didn't keep this from you," I said quietly.

"I know," she replied.

Quick.

Too quick.

"But it still…" She stopped herself, exhaling lightly. "It still shifts things."

Neither of us said anything for a second.

Zion broke the silence, running in. "Mom! You're back!"

Lisa smiled, real, but brief, as she pulled him into a hug.

"I'm back," she said softly.

When she looked up at me again, the smile faded enough to notice.

"We'll figure it out," she said. "One step at a time."

I nodded. "Together."

She didn't repeat it.

***

Breakfast started like any other.

Zion talking.

Plates moving.

Small, normal things filling the space.

But underneath it, something had changed.

Not broken.

Not gone.

Just… unsettled.

And for the first time, I realized this wasn't going to be quick.

Or easy.

Chapter 14

The Shape of What Was Missing

Monday, I arrived quietly, but my thoughts did not. The calm Lisa and I had reached the night before, tentative, fragile, but real, still lingered with me as I sat at my desk, fingers resting idly near my phone. Her choice to step back rather than explode had shifted something in me. It reminded me that love, at its strongest, doesn't always demand answers immediately; it asks for honesty, patience, and courage.

The phone rang.

"Hello," I said, answering my cell phone as I settled into my desk chair Monday morning.

"What's happening, Jacob! Just calling to see how the weekend went with you guys?" Ralph's voice carried a careful curiosity, too measured to be casual.

I knew what he was asking, whether I had told Lisa. Whether the rumor had detonated or quietly lodged itself between us, waiting.

"Man, I couldn't hold it in," I said. "I told her everything. I couldn't look my wife in the eye knowing I was sitting on something like that."

There was a pause at the other end.

"I figured as much," Ralph said. "That couldn't have been easy."

"It wasn't," I admitted. "I wrestled with it all night, paced the floors, replayed the barbershop conversation again. Transparency felt right, but I kept wondering if silence would've spared us both."

I leaned back, staring at the ceiling tiles. Trust, once cracked, never returns to its original shape. You don't rebuild it, you renegotiate it.

"I just want peace," I continued. "Our vow renewal is in two weeks. I can't let something unproven unravel everything we've worked for."

"I hear you," Ralph said. "What do you need from me?"

I exhaled. "I'll backtrack through Zeus and find out where this story started. Somewhere between memory and gossip, there's a truth."

"Say less," he replied. "I'm on it."

The second bell rang in the background, sharp and insistent.

"I've got to go," I said, grabbing my blazer. "Hall duty."

The halls filled quickly, with lockers slamming shut, voices rising, and backpacks dragging across the floor. This space has always grounded me. Here, I wasn't a husband haunted by rumors; I was *Principal Foster*, *present* and *needed*.

I recall a shy young man in the hallway, with rosy cheeks and freckles, named Carter. I often saw him alone, standing unnoticed by the other students during recess or lunch. I soon learned that he felt unwanted because his parents made him feel like a burden due to a learning disability that they were unaware of. He endured cruel taunts, being called "stupid" and other hurtful names that left him feeling deep shame.

I first noticed Carter during a music class. His shoulders were slumped, and his head was down as he held the music score loosely in his hands, softly singing to himself. I could tell this young man had a gift for singing, but he lacked the confidence to project it.

***

After the students left the class, I spoke with Mrs. Simon, their music teacher. She confirmed that Carter had the voice of an angel but lacked confidence.

I made a deal with Carter: I would support him at his concert if he worked hard with Mrs. Simon every day and auditioned for the solo part when the time came. I made an extra effort to speak with him daily to check on his progress. Whenever I needed a break from the office, I would peek through the glass of the music room door to see his confidence grow, little by little. Supporting him through this journey was not just about helping Carter; it was also about rediscovering my own resilience and hope. Watching his confidence blossom inspired me to confront my own challenges with renewed courage, allowing me to find a sense of purpose and fulfillment in being part of his success story.

Finally, on the day of the audition, Carter rushed toward me in the hallway after music class. He exclaimed, "Principal Foster, I did it! I did it! I got the part! I tried out for a solo in my chorus class like you said, and I was selected to lead the song!" He held tightly to the straps of his red backpack, his cheeks glowing with excitement.

"Great job, Carter! I knew you could do it," I said, holding back tears, fully aware of how significant this was for him.

"I must honor my end of the bargain. I will be at your concert with bells on!" I declared proudly.

"Thank you, Mr. Foster! This means the world to me!" he replied, nervously hesitant to hug me before his name was called, as his English teacher summoned him to class.

As the classroom door closed and I returned to my office, I wondered whether my connection with Carter went beyond simply wanting to rescue him; I was also subconsciously seeking to rescue myself.

I spotted Carter near the music room, his shoulders less slumped than they had been before. He caught my eye and nodded, a small but deliberate gesture. Confidence had begun to take root within him.

That's when it hit me. I wasn't drawn to Carter because he needed saving. I was drawn to him because I understood what it felt like to be unseen.

***

By late afternoon, the building was emptied. The resulting silence always felt hard-earned.

I was finishing paperwork when Mrs. Robinson cracked my door open.

"Mr. Foster, Mr. Ralph is on line two. He said it's urgent."

"Transfer him," I said, already standing. "And please remind Mrs. Pridgen I still need Spirit Week themes."

When the line clicked over, Ralph didn't waste time. "I found her."

"Tina?"

"Yes. Social media. It took a while, but I reached her."

"And?"

"She didn't deny anything," he said carefully. "But she wouldn't talk to me. Said she'd been trying to find you, too."

The room felt smaller.

"Ralph," I said, rubbing my forehead, "I just need to know one thing. Is the child mine?"

He exhaled. "That's between you and Tina. She gave me her number for you."

I said nothing.

"One more thing," he added. "Think before you call.

Whatever happens next changes things."

When I got home, Zion was already showered and sprawled on the couch, controller in hand. I retreated to my office, opened my laptop to the social media site, logged on, and stared at the screen longer than I should have.

I typed Tina Beckham's name, each letter feeling weightier than the next with regret, but I had to know.

And then I saw her. *Brianna.*

Her name appeared beneath the photos like a whispered truth. The images themselves were ordinary, college photos typical of campus life, graduation snapshots, and candid moments captured with friends, but something about her presence unsettled me.

It wasn't because she looked like me. It was because she seemed complete. She stood there with quiet confidence, unborrowed and unguarded. This kind of confidence comes from being affirmed and from belonging somewhere without question. I leaned closer, hearing the office chair squeak beneath me. Her skin had a warm chestnut glow, and her almond-shaped, steady eyes held an intelligence sharpened by certainty.

In one photo, she leaned toward the camera, unafraid of being seen. That was what truly unsettled me. I had spent years learning to stand in my own reflection, reconciling the man I had become with the boy I once was. Yet here she was, a young woman whose life had unfolded without my interruption, without my presence, without my protection.

Some mirrors don't show you who you are; they show you who you might have been.

The mirror between us was invisible but undeniable. Each image felt like a quiet accusation, not of wrongdoing, but of absence. I imagined the moments behind the photographs: late-night study sessions, encouragement, and someone showing up.

Even if she wasn't mine, she was someone's answered prayer. And if she were mine, I would have been a missing chapter in a story already written.

I slowly closed the laptop.

I waited for Lisa to come home before making any moves. This truth, whatever it was, didn't belong to me alone.

Chapter 15

The Truth Comes Out

Zion and I were home a few hours when Lisa walked in, shoulders slumped. She rolled her old leather bag in and paused, the strain obvious.

The moment her heels crossed the threshold, Zion and I moved in sync.

We knew the signs.

She slipped off her shoes with a sigh. Her skirt and pearls still neat, she let her hair fall, sinking onto the sofa, spent.

"How'd it go?" I asked.

She exhaled.

"Long. Exhausting. Prep, deadlines, media... But we hit everything."

I smiled. "That's my girl."

She tilted her head toward me. "What about you? You've been quiet."

"It was a good day," I said, and told her about Carter, about the shift I'd seen in him, the confidence starting to take root. I talked longer than I meant to, caught up in something lighter, until her breathing changed.

I glanced over.

She was asleep.

I smiled to myself.

***

Later, as Lisa rested in the living room, Zion came barreling down the hallway moments later, report card in hand, excitement written all over his face.

I held up a finger.

He froze.

Then followed my lead, placing the report quietly on the table before slipping off to grab his reward. When he came back, he draped a blanket over Lisa and kissed her forehead.

Something about that stayed with me.

***

As the evening went on, dinner came together slowly.

Zion helping. Asking questions. Laughing.

Lisa rejoined us after dinner, changed into something comfortable, drawn in by the food and the house's rhythm.

For a while, everything felt... normal.

Almost easy.

But beneath it...

Something waited.

I said, "I have Tina's number." The shift was immediate.

Lisa looked up.

"Is everything alright?" I asked, concerned.

Lisa had been quieter than usual.

Not distant. Just... measured. Every now and then, I'd catch her watching me, not suspicious, not soft either, just thinking.

Like she was still working something out she hadn't said out loud yet.

"We need to talk."

She didn't hesitate.

"Zion, finish in the dining room. Get ready for tomorrow." He nodded, grabbing one last piece of garlic bread as he left.

***

When dinner ended, we stepped onto the patio.

The air was quiet. It didn't urge us along.

"I didn't call her," I said. "Not without you."

Lisa folded her arms, watching me.

A beat passed.

89

"You can call," she said. "From my phone… Speaker."

I nodded.

The phone rang.

Once.

Twice.

Three times.

I nearly hung up.

Then…

"Hello?"

"Tina," I said. "This is Jacob."

A pause.

"I was hoping you'd call."

The conversation moved carefully.

No drama.

No avoidance.

Just truth, slow, steady, and heavier than I expected.

When it ended, the silence that followed felt different.

Not tense.

Just… full.

Lisa reached for the phone.

"Tina," she said gently, "thank you for being honest."

After a pause:

"If Brianna isn't Jacob's, why did people think she was?" Tina answered.

Fear.

Silence.

Survival.

When the call ended, Lisa didn't speak right away.

She just stood there.

Still.

Not frozen, just… present.

Like she had been carrying something all day and had finally set it down.

Then she stepped closer.

"I'm sorry," she said.

I let out a breath I didn't realize I'd been holding. "For what?"

"For letting it get ahead of me. For going somewhere in my head before I had the truth."

I nodded. "I get it."

She pulled back. "No, you handled it right. You told me. You didn't hide anything."

That mattered to her.

I could see it.

The shift.

Not dramatic.

But real.

"We're okay." This time, it didn't feel like reassurance.

It felt like a decision.

We walked back inside together.

Not untouched.

But clearer.

***

Much later, inside the house, it was quiet.

Zion was asleep, his door cracked, light from the hall slipping in. Lisa paused at the frame, steadying herself.

Something real.

Even later that night, we lay side by side in the dark.

No rush to fill the silence.

No need to.

It had changed.

Before drifting off, Lisa spoke softly.

"Let's not carry this into the weekend."

I let out a small breath.

"Deal."

And for the first time in days, my mind didn't race ahead.

It stayed still.

And I slept.

Chapter 16

Surprise, Surprise, Surprise

Lisa and I awoke feeling lighter than we had in weeks. Both of us were off work and filled with gratitude: she for a triumphant presentation, and I for the quiet miracle of reconciliation. By early evening, we were dressed and ready to head downtown to *Johnny P's Prime Seafood and Steak*, which had become our unofficial place of celebration.

As Lisa checked her reflection in the fold-down mirror, she caught me watching her and gave me a smirk.

"What?" she asked.

"Nothing," I said. "Just appreciating the fact that we survived the week."

Lisa laughed, snapped the mirror shut, and slipped her hand into mine. "Let's go enjoy it."

The restaurant was alive, with warm lighting, soft jazz, and the scent of grilled steaks and buttered lobster floating through the air. Ralph and India were already waiting in the lobby, looking relaxed, suspiciously so.

"There they are," Ralph said, pulling me into a half-hug. "The couple who made it through the fire."

Lisa rolled her eyes.

"Please. We're just happy to eat something that didn't come from our kitchen."

India grinned.

"Tonight is about good food and minding everybody else's business."

"That's never been your strength," I said.

She shrugged.

"I contain multitudes."

While we waited to be seated, Lisa and India disappeared toward the ladies' room, an unspoken tradition, leaving Ralph and me standing shoulder to shoulder.

I didn't waste the moment.

"Hey," I said quietly, "I meant what I said earlier this week. I couldn't have gotten through that without you."

Ralph waved it off, but his expression softened.

"That's what brothers are for. And honestly? Watching you and Lisa fight for your marriage, it gives me hope."

"For what?" I asked.

He hesitated, then exhaled. "For something real. I'm tired of building everything except a life."

Before I could respond, the hostess returned, and Lisa and India emerged laughing as if they'd just solved the world's problems.

At the table, chaos resumed immediately.

Ralph accidentally handed India's menu back to the waitress.

"Did you forget I exist?" India asked, craning her neck.

"I remembered," Ralph said. "I just chose violence."

Lisa sighed.

"Why do you two flirt like you're allergic to sincerity?"

"We do not flirt," India snapped.

"You just threatened him with bodily harm," I said

"That's foreplay," India replied.

As drinks arrived and appetizers followed, the banter softened into something warmer. The teasing lingered, but so did the glances, the kind you don't mean to make but don't stop yourself from holding.

When India finally admitted that she and Jerome had ended things, the table fell quiet, not uncomfortably but respectfully.

"That couldn't have been easy," Lisa said.

India shrugged, though her fingers twisted around her glass.

"Some things end so other things can start.

Ralph didn't speak, but I saw the way his posture shifted, hope sneaking in where certainty had lived too long.

Then it happened.

One moment, they were talking. The next, India leaned in and kissed him, quick, decisive, unmistakable.

I nearly fell out of my chair. "HELLO?" I said. "We're still here!"

India leaned back as if nothing had happened. "What? I needed data."

Ralph looked like he'd just won and lost the lottery at the same time.

Lisa shook her head, laughing.

"I leave you alone for five minutes..."

***

As the night wound down, laughter filled the spaces where tension once lived. Watching Ralph and India, awkward, surprised, undeniably drawn, I couldn't help but smile. Watching them, I realized love rarely arrives clean. It arrives awkwardly.

And you decide whether to keep it.

Life had a way of doing that.

Just when you thought the complex parts were over, it handed you something unexpected, not to undo you, but to move you forward. And as we talked about upcoming plans and future gatherings, I had the quiet sense that this, whatever was beginning between them, was only just getting started.

Chapter 17

Where time slips, and grace is briefly given

Isa's voice crackled through my phone, sounding clipped and strained, just as it always did when she was trying to juggle too many things at once.

"Jacob, you are late."

I was running late for our wedding rehearsal, and I again made a poor choice in a chess match against time.

The homecoming game at Franklin had come down to seconds, twenty of them.

We were down by a field goal, the stands alive with

belief and desperation, the marching band frozen mid-song.

I kept telling myself I'd leave after the kickoff, after the snap, after the whistle, but the clock kept bleeding forward, and so did my attention.

"I'm heading to the car now," I said, raising my voice above the roar of the crowd. "I thought I'd be on the road by now."

"Just get here," she replied. I could hear the event planner in the background, rattling off timelines and cues. Then the line went dead.

I didn't need her to say it. I already knew I was in trouble.

I jogged to the parking lot, keys fumbling in my hand, my tie loosened as I slid into the driver's seat. Traffic swallowed me the moment I hit the highway, a slow, crawling procession that pressed against my nerves. When the car ahead of me refused to move from the fast lane, irritation flared hotter than it should have. I honked. He brake-checked me hard.

For a split second, I imagined pulling over and confronting him, but the thought dissolved as quickly as it came. I had somewhere to be. My wife was waiting.

When I finally reached the church exit, relief surged through me, too fast, too reckless.

I rolled through the light, already turning left when the siren cut through the air behind me.

Red and *blue* flooded the car, pulsing against the windshield like a warning I couldn't ignore.

"You've got to be kidding me," I muttered, gripping the wheel.

The officer approached slowly, flashlight sweeping the interior. I kept my hands visible, my pulse loud in my ears.

"Officer Dodson," he said evenly. "You ran that red light back there. License, registration, and insurance."

"I'm on my way to my wedding rehearsal," I said, not as an excuse, more like a plea.

He studied me for a moment, then nodded.

"Sit tight."

As he walked back to his cruiser, I stared straight ahead, thinking of Lisa, of the promise I'd made not to be late, not to let small failures pile into something larger. I thought of how much timing mattered in our life together.

How often did Grace arrive once?

When he returned, he handed me a warning citation.

"Because it's your wedding," he said, tearing the slip from the pad, "I'm letting you off this time. Slow down. Someone could've gotten hurt."

"Thank you," I said, exhaling for what felt like the first time all night.

I drove the rest of the way carefully, reverently, as if every light were sacred.

The chapel doors were already open when I arrived, warm light spilling into the evening. Laughter echoed inside, bridal party voices bouncing off wooden arches polished smooth by decades of vows.

I apologized to everyone before Lisa waved me over, her expression still tight but softened at the edges. The planner reviewed the rehearsal script, pausing to ask if we had any final requests.

"Could we add a moment of silence?" I said. "After the vows."

Lisa turned to look at me, surprised.

"For your parents," I added quietly.

Her throat worked before she nodded.

Lisa had once been Daddy's little girl, fiercely and unapologetically. Losing him during her junior year of college had hollowed her in a way that time never fully repaired. Years later, her mother's sudden death, revealed only after the autopsy, had reinforced a painful lesson: people leave without warning, sometimes without explanation.

The moment of silence wouldn't heal that. But it would

acknowledge the space that was still occupied.

As the rehearsal resumed, Lisa slipped her hand into mine. Her grip was firm, not fragile, but protective. It struck me then how much of her strength came from loss, how instinctively she guarded what she loved.

I promised myself, standing there beneath the chapel lights, that I would never be the one to disappear.

Chapter 18

Unexpected Stranger

S ome truths wait until the night before joy.

The parking lot had emptied by the time the rehearsal ended. As I unlocked my car, I noticed a Buick Century idling a short distance away. The moment my engine turned over, its headlights snapped on.

A ripple of unease moved through me.

The car followed at a steady distance. Each turn I took; it mirrored. I drove past our neighborhood and then pulled into a brightly lit gas station, easing into a pump.

The Buick stopped two lanes over.

Inside the store, I grabbed Zion's favorite snacks and a couple of bottles of the alkaline water Lisa preferred. Standing in line, I felt the earlier tension shift, fear giving way to irritation, irritation hardening into resolve. I reminded myself of who I was, where I came from, and what I could handle.

Back outside, I set the bags in my trunk and approached the Buick, scanning the ground for anything I might use if things went sideways. My gun was at home. *Tonight, I had only instinct.*

I tapped sharply on the window.

The man inside startled, fumbling to turn on the dome light. He was older than I expected, thin, shoulders sloped inward, eyes tired but alert. His hands lifted immediately, palms open.

"I don't mean any harm," he said quickly, rolling the window down.

"Then stop following people," I snapped. "You could've gotten yourself hurt."

He nodded, chastened. "I understand."

"What do you want?" I asked.

"My name is Richard," he said. "I work at the chapel.

"I happened to see you and your wife's picture frame and wedding program as the decoration party was setting up in the foyer earlier today."

Something in his voice, hesitant, weighted, made me pause.

"When I saw your picture near the guest book," he continued, "I thought I was looking at my younger brother."

I frowned.

"I don't think we've met."

"No," he said softly. "But I know your last name."

The word 'name' seemed to linger between us, heavier than it should have.

"Do you know a woman named Ella Foster?" he asked.

"Why?"

"She was involved with my brother," he said. "Years ago. Before he was sent to prison for a crime he didn't commit. She was pregnant when he was taken away," Richard said. "He was exonerated recently. All he's ever wanted since is to know his son."

The world seemed to tilt, just slightly.

"You're saying?" I began.

"I'm saying you should ask your mother," he replied gently. "That's all."

He scribbled his number on a scrap of paper and held it out to me, his hand trembling, not with fear, but with age.

"I didn't want to disturb you tonight," he said.

"Tomorrow's important. I didn't know if I'd ever see you again."

Yet beneath it all was something else, an echo I couldn't yet name. The sense that the silence passed down had a way of resurfacing. That life intersected whether we were ready or not.

When I pulled into the driveway, the house lights were on. Tomorrow, I will stand at an altar and promise transparency, presence, and permanence.

Tonight, I folded the paper carefully and slipped it into my wallet, close to my heart, where unanswered things tend to live.

Chapter 19

Where joy arrives without asking permission

The long-awaited wedding day finally arrived. On our way to the wedding venue, Zion's happiness was contagious as he talked about the honor of walking his mother down the aisle instead of his grandfather.

The weather was more than perfect. The gentle sunshine and clear skies set the ideal romantic backdrop for our wedding day. This day was not just a new beginning but a fresh start to a better future, and I was ready for it.

Meanwhile, Lisa was at home with Elizabeth, our event

planner, the hairstylist, and the rest of the bridal party, all working together to make this day one we will remember forever.

I parked at the side entrance and called Elizabeth to check if Lisa had received my surprise.

"Mr. Jacob, how are you?" Elizabeth greeted me cheerfully. In her mid-40s, she was one of the best high-end event planners around, and we truly appreciated her expertise in making today as unique as possible.

"I am excited to see Lisa in her wedding gown for the first time after such a long wait. While saying 'I do' in front of the Justice of the Peace was nice, exchanging our vows in front of our friends and family will make it feel even more special, especially since Zion is now old enough to participate," I shared.

"Totally get that!" she replied, clearly excited for us.

"Have the bouquet of long-stem roses and the card.

I ordered arrived yet?" I asked, my heart racing with anticipation. I knew that thoughtful surprises like this always warmed her heart.

"They arrived about ten minutes ago. Let me tell you, Lisa is still talking about them and telling the girls how kind and thoughtful you are. That was a great move, Jacob," Elizabeth said confidently.

She shared that Lisa's eyes had sparkled with tears of joy when she first saw the bouquet.

"Such a beautiful surprise!" she exclaimed, clutching the roses with joy, her voice trembling with emotion. Hearing her delight was a moment I'll treasure forever.

Hearing her voice in the background was like a sweet love song, taking me back to the moment we first met.

"Get your handkerchief ready! You won't believe how beautiful Lisa looks! The stylist just finished retouching her hair, and the makeup artist is currently applying her makeup." Elizabeth did her best to describe the scene of Lisa's preparations to me.

"My heart is about to jump out of my chest. You don't know how long I've been waiting for this day." I said. "We truly appreciate the phenomenal job you've done thus far."

"My clients' happiness is important. We will see you soon! I must get back to ensure everything is going according to plan," she responded before hanging up to return to her tasks.

I turned off the ignition and opened the car door, checking the distance between my car and Ralph's as he pulled up.

We approached each other at the back of our vehicles, exchanging our signature handshake and sportsmanlike hug as Zion looked on. Ralph greeted Zion and complimented him on his sharp haircut before checking in on me.

"So, how do you feel, man?" Ralph asked.

"I'm feeling good! It's a new day, the sun is shining, and I am renewing my vows with the woman I love even more. I have my son, who is healthier than ever…and my best friend on our special day. What more could a man ask for?" I replied, looking up at the open sky.

Ralph opened his trunk to get his things, while Zion helped me with our belongings, grabbing my leather toiletry bag, which contained my brush, cologne, and other essentials, and my tuxedo shoes. I picked up the suit bag that held our tuxedos.

We walked toward the antique, engraved wooden double doors of the chapel. The landscape was breathtaking, with freshly cut grass bordered by pink and lavender tulips. A vibrant array of colorful flowers lined the curving, ancient stone walkway.

Our footsteps echoed through the marble-floored hallway as we approached our dressing room door. We hung our garment bag, began organizing our personal belongings, and took out our tuxedos to change.

I reached into my bag and took out the three-carat ring for Lisa and my wedding band, both carefully stored in a black velvet case. I placed the rings in Ralph's hand for safekeeping, knowing that his role in the preparations was crucial. Then, I called Zion from across the room to help him put on his tuxedo. Once dressed, Ralph used a lint roller to inspect our outfits. The event planner's assistant then called Zion to review his role in the wedding.

"You look great, Dad!" Zion said, giving me a thumbs up.

"Thank you, son. You look sharp yourself." I said as he followed the assistant. I adjusted my bowtie in the mirror for one last time.

"Well, this is it!" I said within myself.

"Jacob, it's time. Are you ready, man?" Ralph asked, placing his hand on my shoulder.

"As ready as I'll ever be," I replied.

"I'm so happy that you guys are finally having the ceremony you always dreamed of."

"After what we've been through the last few weeks, it challenged us in ways I never thought of. I thought for a moment it was close to being over, but God looked out for us, and I am a better man because of it."

I poured myself a glass of ice water and settled into one of the vintage wingback chairs by the window. My mind raced with all the experiences we had shared, each one leading us to this special moment.

Meanwhile, Ralph began patting down his pockets, searching for his car keys, with about forty minutes to spare as family and guests arrived.

"Ah, man, I left the handkerchiefs in my truck. I'll be back," he said, reaching for his keys to his Land Rover before leaving me alone with my thoughts in the room.

A few minutes passed before there was a gentle knock on the door.

"Come on in," I responded.

"Jacob?" India walked in, wearing an elegant navy-blue mermaid-style bridesmaid dress. Small flowers were strategically placed in her now auburn sister's locks, which were styled in a fancy updo.

"Oh, there you are!" she exclaimed, finding me by the tapestry window and vintage bookshelves.

"India, the closer and closer we get, the more anticipation I have to see her in that beautiful gown," I spoke.

"All I've got to say is to prepare your handkerchief and break out the defibrillator, because Lisa is about to take your breath away!" India said, snapping her fingers.

As if on cue, Ralph hustled into the room, turning India's attention.

"*Whoa!* You are gorgeous in that dress," Ralph said, stopping in his tracks.

"Did you lose something?" India asked. Ralph stood motionless.

"I think I did. I lost my parking ticket!" Ralph shot back.

"Parking ticket?" India responded by raising an eyebrow.

"Yeah, a parking ticket. And you helped me find it, because you have 'fine' written all over you!" he quipped.

"Ralph, that was so lame," I said, laughing hysterically. "Is that really your best pick-up line? You didn't have anything better to say?"

"I think it was cute. His game needs a lot of work, but the tuxedo and the smell of his cologne make up for it," India replied in compliment.

"Thank you! But as lovely as you are, who needs the sun when you're around?" Ralph said, captivated by her beauty.

He took her hand and slowly turned her around to admire her, his eyes taking in every detail from head to toe.

I stood and waved at them both, interrupting his gaze.

"Hey, guys! I'm still in the room, you know, and this is my ceremony!" I chuckled.

"Relax, Jacob, and stop hating all the time. I have that touch!" India laughed.

"Yes, you do!" Ralph exclaimed, unable to contain himself as he shook his head, mumbling under his breath as she walked away. "Man, did you see that walk, bro?" Ralph was fixed on the door as she left.

"Naw, man! I don't look at her like that!" I replied jokingly.

"Yeah, well, I do!!!" Ralph said, tucking his handkerchief into his top pocket.

"Are you two even together?" I asked.

"I'm not sure," Ralph said, looking up at the ceiling thoughtfully.

"If you're not ready to deal with a shark, you might want to stick with the little goldfish you can handle," I said. "You know as well as I do that India doesn't play, as you recall between you two at the restaurant. I've seen a couple of guys she dropped like a bad habit, without a second thought."

India, with her sharp wit and independent spirit, was not someone to be underestimated. India then chimed in with a playful grin, "Well, I guess I'm the shark in this water, but if *yo'* boy is ready, he needs to let me know." India said to me, knowing Ralph was within earshot. Her humor cut through the room, and even Ralph couldn't help but chuckle, clearly enjoying the lively exchange.

"Yeah, but none of the men she dated were in her league. You see, once you get past that tough exterior, I'm sure she's the most loving and kind woman a man could ever know. In a way, that tough exterior is a good thing because it wards off the weak."

"At the same time, that tough exterior can also keep love away," I replied. "I don't want to say that Lisa was that way, but... "

"...But she was that way. Just go ahead and say it, man," Ralph retorted.

"I will neither confirm nor deny that fact," I smiled.

"I love a challenge, especially from a strong woman like India."

"So, why haven't you made your move yet? You two seem to be dating other people, and, ironically, you end up single at the same time. That might be a sign, man. She already kissed you at the restaurant, and she did say that when she wants something, she takes it." I laughed. "You two need to get married after us today!" We both broke out in laughter. "India may be the woman you need. You never know unless you try."

"This is going to be an exciting journey, indeed!" Ralph replied, ready for the challenge.

Chapter 20

Where truth stands in the light

The atmosphere was charged with anticipation as guests settled into their seats, their whispers blending with soft instrumental music. All attention was focused on the front as the moment we had all been waiting for was about to unfold.

The cathedral ceilings bore sparkling chandeliers that glistened as rays of light shone through the tapestry windows. You could hear the shuffling of feet on the limestone cabochon floor among the decorative wedding columns, which were filled with fluffy white roses that adorned each antique chestnut oak pew, making them even more brilliant as sunlight bounced off the walls of the wedding venue. At the top of the chapel's interior were masterfully designed chestnut oak pillars. The plethora of white floating votive candles on stands throughout the sanctuary contributed to the romantic atmosphere.

"Here and Now," by Luther Vandross signaled the ceremony party's entrance. The groomsmen swaggered slowly into the sanctuary, majestic in starched tuxedos, accompanied by a bridesmaid in a beautiful coral-blue version of the floor-length mermaid dress India wore as the maid of honor. I struggled to keep a consistent breathing pattern as a brief pause ensued as I took my place at the altar.

The music played as the doors opened in radiance, with Lisa standing still and Zion by her side. Lisa walked down the narrow aisle. The light shining behind her made her look like an angel in her beautiful designer wedding gown, shimmering with pearls. My palms began to sweat, my stomach churned, and my pulse quickened as the doors opened for her entrance. Everyone stood in unison; the heavy sound of the benches and shuffling feet echoed in my ears like an army of marching soldiers. Cell phones at the ready, they pivoted their bodies as the preacher announced her entrance. I could no longer hold back my tears.

Thankfully, Ralph gave me two handkerchiefs, one for me and one for Lisa.

I stood in awe as my wife walked down the aisle. Zion proudly escorted her in honor of his grandpa, whom he never got the opportunity to meet. Though his face was determined, I could see the nervous excitement in his eyes as he straightened his tie one last time before taking those careful steps.

In that moment, gratitude for Zion washed over me as he stepped into shoes, twice his size. A role deeply meaningful to Lisa and to us all. His quiet strength comforted us, and I knew how much this gesture would have meant to Lisa's father.

Her train trailed gracefully behind.

Through my tear-blurred eyes, she was an angel, a glowing white silhouette of pearls. I joined her at the altar, nodding to Zion in thanks. No eyes were dry. The months leading up to this day had challenged our faith and trust. Standing together now, we felt the weight of what we had overcome and the hope that guided us here.

Looking deeply into her eyes, I whispered that she was beautiful as I wiped away her tears.

She, in turn, wiped mine.

Afterward, we turned towards Reverend Moore as he motioned for the congregation to take their seats.

***

"Dearly beloved, we are gathered here today to witness the renewal of wedding vows between Jacob and Lisa Foster." His voice echoed.

"After ten years of watching these two grow, I have personally witnessed the positive changes in both of their lives.

As they already know, marriage is not easy; it involves the merging of two lives, which can sometimes lead to friction. However, I am grateful that whenever the road got a little rough, this young man and woman reached out to my wife and me, saying, *'Pastor Moore, after fifty years of marriage, how did you handle this problem or that problem?'* I would encourage them to seek God first and always be honest and transparent, no matter how painful it might be. For you see, beloved, it is better to tell the truth and be forgiven than to lie and deceive, because that is not love. 1 Corinthians 13:7 says that love always protects, always trusts, always hopes, and always perseveres. I pray that they will continue to nurture and protect their love, marriage, and family." He concluded with a heartfelt prayer and blessing for us.

"Now, Lisa and Jacob would like to share the vows they have prepared for each other. Lisa, please go first," Reverend Moore said.

The atmosphere in the wedding chapel was so serene that even the softest sounds seemed amplified. In the hushed reverence of the moment, muffled coughs echoed faintly, while the delicate sound of someone sniffing could be heard in the background.

Lisa took both of my hands in hers, her hands so soft and warm. She looked into my eyes, drawing me into the atmosphere of feeling that everything around me had vanished except her.

"Jacob, I love you. I appreciate you *so* much. We have experienced so many things together. As Reverend Moore said, I agree that our path was not always easy, but you never left my side. When we first met, I never knew how much I needed you, but looking back now, I can't see my life without you. You came and opened my eyes to so much more. Thank you for being patient with my hurts. You bring me comfort when I am afraid. And when I lost my mother..." Lisa paused to catch her breath as tears fell. "...you were there to hold me." Lisa's voice began to tremble. "Through the grieving process and even now when I miss her, still, there has never been a time you haven't made yourself available to comfort me. You're such a great father and the perfect example of a man to our son," she said, as I reached for my handkerchief to wipe my eyes as she continued.

"God exceeded what I wished for in a man. Jacob, I commit my heart, my soul, my everything to you again, and pray that God will continue to help me be the woman He called me to be in your life. Thank you for being our protector, our greatest supporter, and the best husband any woman could ever pray for." Lisa concluded.

I took a deep breath, taking in everything Lisa said.

Overwhelmed with emotion, Zion and I were both wiping tears from our eyes.

"I can do this," I said, letting out a laugh of mixed emotion. Ralph reached around my shoulder to hand me another handkerchief, noticing the first was already soaked with tears.

"Ok. Here we go." I exhaled heavily, hearing now audible awes, sporadic sniffs, and noses being blown throughout the crowd.

"A man who finds a wife finds a good thing and obtains favor from the Lord. Lisa, I want the world to know today that I found both of those things in you ten years ago. When I first met you, I'll be honest, I didn't feel qualified. I thought I was wounded beyond repair and was sure you wouldn't even give me the time of day. But you did. You saw me. On the outside, everyone saw a strong, confident man, a man who had more compassion for others than for myself, but you saw me. You saw my heart, saw my mistakes, and even understood my tears. You never judged me, and you never made me feel like less of a man. You showed me grace. Although you can be a little rough around the edges at times and sometimes brutally honest, I have learned to appreciate that quality in you. I never thought I would find a woman like you. Since the day we met, I have not stopped showing God how thankful I am for bringing you into my life and being married to a woman as special as you. You are a dream come true. I vow to love you until my last breath. I vow to return all you have given me a hundredfold. Lisa, I love you. My world would not be complete without you. I vow to be the man you need, to support you, and to do all I can to help you fulfill God's plan for your life. You are everything to me. I love you so much." I concluded as we both turned to Reverend Moore, who motioned for Ralph to hand him the rings for the ceremony.

After explaining their purpose, he blessed the rings and gave them to us for the formal portion of the renewal of our vows.

"Jacob, do you solemnly promise to continue to love, cherish, and honor her, in sickness and in health, respect, and pledge your life to her until God, by death, shall separate you?" Reverend Moore asked.

"I do," I said.

"Lisa, will you take Jacob to be your wedded husband? Do you promise before God and these witnesses, to love, honor, and respect him in sickness and in health, performing the duties of a wife unto her husband, until God, by death, shall separate you?"

"I will," Lisa responded.

"Let us pray," Reverend Moore said. "Father, I thank You

for these two precious people. Let the love they share grow even stronger than before. Let each challenge be a stepping-stone for growth, as you give them the grace to fulfill the vows they have said to one another before Your presence, here today. In the name of the Father and of the Son and of the Holy Spirit, Amen." Reverend Moore said, "Amen," followed by a moment of silence in tribute to Lisa's parents.

"You may salute your wife." He continued with a smile.

I kissed Lisa with overwhelming love and warmly embraced her, our love radiating through the room.

The audience erupted in a standing ovation, their joy palpable as Lisa and I walked down the aisle with Zion. The wedding party followed behind, ready to capture the joy in traditional wedding photos.

After our photos, we exited the sanctuary and hopped into the 1951 white glistening Rolls-Royce. The car was decorated with white silk ribbons, swinging from the hood emblem to each side of the windowpane. The bridesmaids helped me delicately fold Lisa's long wedding gown train into the vehicle to keep it from getting dirty.

Lisa's head never left my shoulder during our journey to the reception. I couldn't help but notice the sparkles of her cheeks as she continued to glow.

I looked down at our intertwined hands. Seeing her ring

finger deepened my resolve even more to be the best husband and supporter she would always need. As Lisa rested her head on my shoulder, it felt like more than a simple gesture; it symbolized our shared release from the pain and disappointments of our past.

At that moment, I sensed our love had been given new life.

Chapter 21

The Reception

Lisa and I decided to sneak away to our deluxe suite for a private moment before the reception. On the king-sized bed was a tray of fresh strawberries dipped in fine chocolate, with two intertwined roses resting on soft white and earth-toned pillows.

Lisa's eyes sparkled. "This room is gorgeous!" She kicked off her heels and paced around like a child, gazing out at the tall windows at the city view.

"I'm glad you like it," I said, drinking in the sight of her.

Sunlight highlighted the smooth radiance of her skin, and I found myself captivated by the elegance of her stance, the soft curves that seemed sculpted by an artist's hand.

I slipped off my tuxedo jacket and moved behind her, wrapping my arms around her waist. I inhaled the sweet scent of her perfume.

"You are so beautiful," I whispered, kissing her softly behind the ear.

"That tickles," Lisa giggled, turning her cheek toward my lips. She leaned in, and our lips met in a tender kiss.

"What about the guests and the reception?" she murmured playfully. I grinned. Nothing felt more urgent than staying here with her a little longer.

"Don't worry," I reassured her. "I planned forty-five minutes of entertainment for the guests downstairs."

My fingers traced from her shoulders down her arms as I gazed into her mischievous eyes before leaning in for another kiss.

"You're going to have to wait, tiger," she teased, sliding onto the bed with her legs crossed elegantly.

"Good things come to those who wait," she added, her eyes sparkling with mischief.

We finally made our way downstairs to the atrium, greeted by warm applause. Lisa blushed, smiling as we thanked our guests.

Elizabeth approached with the seating diagram.

"About thirty minutes of waiting, but we're ahead of schedule," she said.

I joked with Lisa, and she laughed, planting a kiss on my cheek. To pass the time, we chatted with Ralph and India, sharing memories and our honeymoon plans for Fiji.

The DJ cued "Fantastic Voyage" by Lakeside.

Flashing cameras welcomed us as we danced our way into the ballroom. Lisa laughed as I performed my robot and breakdancing moves, both of us feeling like kids again.

After the dance, we settled at the head table. Ivory drapery and coral-and-navy candles framed the space, with swan ice sculptures and a three-tiered white fondant cake adorned with edible roses. Lisa marveled at the decor.

Ralph raised a toast, sharing childhood stories that had me squirming with embarrassment. "Jacob once wanted to be a professional wrestler," he said, recounting my days as "The Brown Hornet."

I nudged him to hurry, and he finished with heartfelt words, toasting to our happiness. India followed with a humorous toast, eliciting laughter from Lisa and everyone else.

Guests shared their wishes, we cut the cake, and laughter filled the ballroom. Classic dance tunes played as the bouquet was tossed, caught, ironically, by India.

Finally, exhaustion crept in as the night wound down.

Lisa and I retreated to our suite, where fresh rose petals and candlelight awaited, a secret touch I had arranged.

Inside, we kissed passionately.

The romantic music and dimmed lights framed our intimacy as we gave ourselves entirely to one another, every touch and kiss spoke of love, commitment, and the beginning of our shared lives.

Chapter 22

Family Matters

Enjoying our honeymoon bliss, we decided to take the day off to recover from our honeymoon weekend and spend Monday together as a family. I had already informed Zion's teacher about his absence. Still, I wanted to ensure he wouldn't miss out on meeting his classmates and friends during their field trip to the Trampoline and Adventure Park.

That morning, we called my mother to let her know we were on our way to pick up Zion. While we enjoyed our brief honeymoon at the hotel, Zion thrived at Grandmother Ella's house. Being her only grandchild, he was spoiled with cookies, games, and laughter. She allowed him to be a kid, far removed from the polished expectations of our neighborhood.

By the time we arrived at my mother's house on Hasty Street, Zion was eagerly anticipating our reunion. The three-bedroom, two-bathroom brick home, shaded by two towering trees, radiated comfort, and its flower garden showed evidence of careful attention.

As I rang the doorbell, I could hear the muffled sound of my mother's new flat-screen TV leaking through the walls. When she opened the door, her warm and unshakeable smile greeted us. "It's so good to see you! Come in!" she exclaimed.

Lisa and I stepped inside, embraced by the familiar warmth of home. Watching Zion prepare to leave, I felt a pang of contrast between his carefree anticipation and my own childhood, where such moments were rare and fleeting. This shared family time was a gift, a reminder of how far we'd come and the memories I wanted to create for my son.

As Lisa and Zion gathered his things, I took a moment to notice the changes in my mother's home. The picture frames that had once adorned her old TV stand were gone, replaced by a new entertainment center and a leather couch set.

"Where did the photo frames go?" I asked, feeling nostalgic.

"Inside a box, along with the old albums," she said. "I meant to take them to the garage, but… well, I keep forgetting."

I offered to take them. Zion helped carry the albums and the box, though the weight proved tricky. One toppled to the garage floor with a loud thud, spilling photographs and sending the faint scent of aged paper into the air. A wave of memory hit me, and I paused, remembering the hours my mother and I spent looking through these very albums, telling stories that stitched my past together.

As Zion explored the photos, asking about the people in vintage fashion, I gently guided him, showing him a picture of me as a boy.

"That's me," I said.

He studied it intently.

"Were you and Grandma poor?" he asked, innocence and curiosity in equal measure.

"We had our struggles," I admitted. "But God always provided. That's why I'm grateful for where we are now."

Flipping through the albums, my eyes settled on a group photo: my mother flanked by two young men. The man on her left was Richard. I recognized him immediately; his features mirrored those I remembered. To her right stood another man, my father, his presence unmistakable. The need to understand surged within me, and I went inside to confront my mother privately.

"What took you so long?" Lisa asked as I handed her the car keys.

"Just a moment," I replied. I showed my mother the photo, who paused, recognition flickering in her eyes.

"Who are these two men?" I asked.

"They're old friends," she said, but her hesitation betrayed her words.

I pressed gently, "One of them is Richard Jones. And the other?"

"He's your father," she said quietly.

"Then why hide him from me all these years?" I asked, my voice low but steady.

Fear and love mixed in her expression.

"I was scared. Scared you might become like him. I loved you too much to risk that. I thought…," mother hesitated, "I thought it was safer to declare him gone."

Her confession wrapped around me like a delicate thread of understanding.

She had acted from love, even amid fear and hardship.

"Did he treat you worse than Sledge?" I asked softly.

"Yes…especially when he drank. One personality: Sober; another: a monster.

I stayed because I was young, pregnant, and hoping he'd change. But he never did. One day, I finally left…and then, a week later, he was arrested."

Her relief and sorrow intertwined, palpable and raw.

I took her hand, kissing her forehead.

"Thank you, Mom. For everything you endured, for me, for us."

Tears shimmered in her eyes.

"I love you so much, my son. Seeing you smile gave me a reason to fight when I had none."

Lisa peeked in, unaware of the depth of our conversation. Zion was already restless, eager to join his friends.

"We'll see you later, Mom. Call me if you need anything," I said, giving her a reassuring smile as we left, our hearts full yet tinged with reflection.

Chapter 23

Remember When

My thoughts drifted back to my conversation with my mother as we drove to the trampoline park earlier that morning. I could still picture the concern in her eyes, the way her voice trembled as she responded to my question. In that moment, feeling overwhelmed, I reacted impulsively, and now I couldn't shake the feeling that I might have inadvertently hurt her. I hoped I hadn't broken her heart; it pained me to think she felt that way because of my response.

Lisa and Zion's laughter and animated conversation

contrasted sharply with my quiet introspection. They were catching up on his weekend with Grandma Ella and all the fun things they did together, which made me feel even worse.

The car radio played softly in the background, offering snippets of upbeat music that mirrored their enthusiasm. I tried to join the conversation from time to time, tossing in a comment here and there, not to disturb their cheerful exchange but to subtly remind them of my presence.

Despite my attempts to engage, my thoughts were elsewhere, drifting like clouds across a summer sky, pulled away from the moment and into a sea of my own reflections and worries. The vibrant atmosphere around me felt almost surreal as I battled my inner dialogue, while they reveled in their shared memories.

***

We finally arrived at the Trampoline and Adventure Park. Once inside the building, we were welcomed by the laughter and cheers of four busloads of elementary school students from Zion's Elementary School. He spotted a group of his friends and asked for permission to join them. On the other hand, we focused on receiving his makeup assignments from his teacher, who was quite eager to hear about how the ceremony went. According to her, Zion talked about it in his class, saying he was ready to escort Lisa down the aisle in his tuxedo.

"Zion, be careful out there, okay? We don't want you to get hurt," Lisa said with a worried look as he dashed around the trampoline area, chasing after his classmates. "I hope he's going to be alright," she added, giving me a concerned glance.

"He's a kid! They bounce back quickly. Plus, a few little bumps and bruises will toughen him up a bit," I replied with a smile.

"Are you sure about that? I swear I heard your knees cracking like popcorn when you knelt to fix Zion's shoelaces! Is that the toughness you're talking about?" Lisa teased, her eyes twinkling with mischief.

"What are you trying to say? We can head over to the jousting platform and settle this right now!" I laughed, enjoying the playful banter. Lisa took me up on my challenge as we walked over and stood in line.

"Excuse me, young lady," Lisa said cheerfully to the attendant in charge of the jousting game. "I'm guessing you have an EMT on standby because my husband is going to need one after I take him down!"

We were both feeling competitive, and it had been a while since we'd challenged each other, so we were more than ready for some lighthearted fun.

"Oh no, you're the one who's going to need them!" I shot back playfully as we grabbed our jousting beams and took our places. The young lady supervising was laughing as we continued to exchange friendly jabs. Zion and his classmates glanced over, amused, and cheered us on. For a moment, it felt great to let go and reminisce about being kids again.

Just before the whistle blew, Lisa scored a sneaky hit while I was busy entertaining the kids. BAM! She struck me on the side of my head with enough force to make me lose my balance and tumble into the pile of blue and green cushions.

"Hey, that was such a cheap shot!" I laughed, looking up at Lisa as she celebrated her win.

"You should have been paying more attention!" she teased.

I couldn't resist. I jumped up from the cushion pit, grabbed her leg, and pulled her in with me. We started tossing the cubed cushions at each other, giggling all the while. As we climbed out of the jousting pit, I heard one of the kids say to Zion, "Your parents are funny, but they're also really cool!" That brought smiles to everyone's faces. Zion beamed in agreement.

Zion's class was called to the table for pizza at lunch, signaling that it was time to leave for the mall to shop and eat.

"Are you hungry too, buddy?" I asked with a smile.

"I'm starving!" Zion replied.

"Let's go get something to eat!" "Where are we going, Dad?"

"To the mall! We'll grab a bite to eat and pick out a gift for your mom from both of us. Sounds good?"

"That sounds awesome!" Zion said, waving goodbye to his classmates as they left the building.

"Hey, Dad, could I also get some new headphones for my game?" he asked hopefully.

"I see what you're doing there, taking advantage of the moment! That's a smart move, future businessman!" Zion was smarter than I thought. "Alright, since you pulled a fast one on me, you can get the headphones, but you'll need to use your money," I chuckled as we climbed into the car, on our way to the mall.

After we finally satisfied our appetites at Chick-fil-A, I paused for a moment, my gaze fixating on a nearby table as a wave of nostalgia washed over me.

"Did you forget something?" Lisa asked, turning to me with a look of concern, thinking I had left my keys behind on the table.

I grinned, enjoying the playful moment. "You don't remember?" I replied, my eyes sparkling with mischief.

"Remember what?" she inquired, feigning innocence.

With a warm smile, I reflected on the past. "This very table is where I first bumped into your mother while I was enjoying my lunch. We were getting to know each other at the time, long before you were even thought of," I explained to Zion.

"Oh, yeah. Now I recall," Lisa said, her face turning a deep shade of red as the memories flooded back to her. "I was taking my lunch break from work to come shop for a few things at the mall, little did I know your father was also having lunch here. He was sitting at this table, his muscles almost bursting out of his shirt as he devoured chicken nuggets with a cup of diet lemonade. He looked incredibly handsome that day," she said, her voice softening with nostalgia as she recounted the moment. "I was so happy to see him, knowing our lunch meeting was completely unplanned. Looking back now, I believe it was a sign from God."

Zion's expression shifted as his eyes widened, captivated by the vivid imagery her words conjured. He was fully engrossed, his imagination running wild as he envisioned his parents as carefree individuals falling in love over chicken nuggets.

We left the food court and strolled to where I needed to buy Zion's headphones, then surprised Lisa with a memorable trip to the Christian Louboutin Boutique.

"No way!" Lisa said as we approached. "Yes *way*," I replied with joy.

Lisa couldn't wait to head straight for the heels she had always dreamed of. The joy on her face when she tried them on was like a beautiful sunrise, warming my heart and making me think about adding the matching purse. Overwhelmed with happiness, she wrapped her arms around Zion and me, thanking us for the thoughtful gift.

"Jacob, I was going to ask for these for Christmas!" she exclaimed.

"Well, I guess Christmas came a little early for you, huh?" I replied with a grin, and Lisa dove in for another hug.

I knew Lisa was excited, not because we couldn't afford it, but because we could! Her joy reflected her kind spirit, always putting others first.

At the register, she glanced at the total and whispered, "Are you sure, babe? This money could go toward other things we need, like a fun family vacation."

"Don't worry, everything is all set. I promise I've got this," I said, pulling out my credit card, paying without second thought.

"I've had my eyes on this set forever!" Lisa smiled, opening the bags once more before I closed the trunk.

"I can't tell you how many times I've seen you admiring them on your Pinterest account," I laughed. "I had to do something special for you right now."

"You surprised me!" Lisa's eyes sparkled with happiness, lighting up my day.

Where it all Began

While we enjoyed our time together as a family, a wave of nostalgia washed over me. As we laughed and shared stories about my childhood, sparked by the pictures my child had seen at his grandmother's house, I realized it would be a good idea to show him those places in person. I wanted him to see my humble beginnings and understand that nothing in life comes without effort.

Neither Lisa nor Zion had ever seen where I lived, except through pictures. I thought it would be a good idea to show them in person, which made Lisa, who came from an upper-class family, very nervous, but she trusted me anyway.

As we entered South Dallas, I pointed out many landmarks I used to visit by transit with my mother when I was younger. Lisa gazed at the scene around her, taking in the low-income housing, crumbling buildings, and homeless individuals wandering the streets like zombies.

"When you were sharing stories about your childhood, I had to confess that I thought you might be embellishing a bit. I never expected the area to look this way." Lisa said, her eyes filled with amazement and unease.

"I almost forgot how rough it was out here," I said, the memories flooding back. The stores and houses, once so familiar and tidy, were now covered in graffiti and gang signs. "It's a miracle that Ralph and I managed to escape this. I can't even recognize our old neighborhood."

I pointed to the abandoned small corner stores where we used to buy soda pop, Lemonheads, and Boston Baked Beans, to the locations where we would gather cardboard boxes in the '80s to hold breakdancing contests, and to the local barbershops. We drove further into the city, passing more trap houses with spray-painted plywood for windows and broken-down cars decorating their front lawns like tiny junkyards.

What was once a hard-working, blue-collar community had become a desolate ghost town due to economic decline and city neglect. Factory closures left many unemployed, leading to a rise in poverty. I could tell the city officials couldn't have cared less about the community now that all the factories had shut down after jobs were shipped overseas at lower costs, leaving crime unchecked. I imagined Nightfall would signal the Phantom of the Opera of the streets: the occasional crackle of gunfire echoing down the streets, accompanied by music filled with profanity blaring from 808 bass sound systems that rattled as they cruised slowly by.

As I parked in front of our old house, I couldn't help but feel a wave of emotions.

"Here we are," I said to Lisa, my voice tinged with nostalgia and sadness. The sight of the empty, dilapidated house brought back memories of the day my stepfather left my mother and me standing alone in the yard. It was a memory I had long avoided, but now it has resurfaced, forcing me to confront it head-on.

"Are you okay?" Lisa asked, gently touching my arm, sensing my hesitation in what now felt like an unfamiliar place.

"I'll be right back. I want to take a closer look since it's been years since I've been out here," I said, motioning for Lisa to stay in the car. I hit the lock button on my key fob as an extra safety precaution.

Scanning the yard, which was filled with dust, stray cats, and patches of dry grass, I approached the sidewalk and traced the rusty chain-link fence with my hand. I struggled to open the gate because the overgrown vines had consumed the concrete porch and chipped away at the house's worn wooden paneling.

Standing before the detached screen door, I could hear my mother's voice calling out to the younger me to straighten up my room and pull down the green-framed shutter window before I went to sleep, especially on a smoldering school night. Zion asked my wife if he could get out and come with me.

"Well, maybe we should remain in the car." She slowly reached to check that the door was still locked as she scanned the neighborhood, which looked like a horror movie set.

"Aw, Mom," Zion sighed disappointedly. I turned to see the look on his face and changed my mind, heading back to the car to take him with me.

"C'mon, babe, we may not be able to come back for quite some time. Let's give him a chance to experience a little of what it was like for me growing up. I won't let him leave my sight." Before we knew it, Zion unlocked the door and leaped out to join me on the sidewalk.

"Please keep an eye on *my* child," Lisa said as I closed the door behind him and locked it.

"Don't you mean *our* child?" I teased her, giving her a reassuring smile.

"Yes, yes, but please hurry. This is starting to feel a little

spooky, and I'm getting chill bumps being in this neighborhood."
Lisa rechecked the car door as I walked with Zion, holding his
hand.

"Be careful, son, make sure you stay close to me, alright?" I
said, my protective instincts kicking in as Zion nodded in
agreement.

"Look, Dad, that's the spot where you took the picture in
front of the house as a little boy," Zion pointed at the yard.

"That's right, it is! I used to practice my Michael Jackson
moves right by that tree." I pointed. "It wasn't as overgrown and
old as it is now," I said with a sense of deep connection to my
childhood home.

We could not go any further because an old, rusty fence
installed shortly after moving blocked the way. A *No Trespassing*
sign, attached by a paper-thin wire, dangled loosely, making a
slight tapping noise with each passing breeze. We could barely
see the house through all the junk in the yard, including old
cardboard boxes, trash, and scattered beer bottles.

There was no doubt this house, once lovingly cared for and
filled with love, was now lonely and neglected. *Dead.* The only
item missing was crime tape to seal the deal. My heart sank at the
sight; a mixture of sadness and disbelief came over me.

I did my best to engage his creative insight beyond what we
could see before we had to leave. I pointed out all the places in
the yard where I used to go to think and escape, hoping to create a

safe space for him.

I had the opportunity to tell him about our struggles and how I became responsible by helping people in the neighborhood, in addition to my regular chores of washing dishes and clothes. I made money selling Coca-Cola bottles, collecting cans, and I had a newspaper route. When it was too hot outside to play, I would plug the Atari 2600 into the tiny television and play games like Q-Bert, Asteroids, Centipede, and Donkey Kong. I laughed at the confused expression on his face as I described these 80's video games, as if I were speaking Chinese.

"Come on, son, it's time to go. I guess that's enough for now," I said, moving from the fence towards the car. "But I'm not done yet, daddy," he protested, his fingers still clinging to the fence as he scanned the yard with intrigue.

"I promise, I'll tell you more tonight. Your mother is getting worried we've been out here too long already, and I think it's also a smart idea for us to leave before it gets too dark," I ushered him to his side of the car as he got in. Lisa's relief at our departure from the district was evident.

I kept my promise to answer the rest of Zion's questions on the way home. Taking him to my old neighborhood would let him see firsthand that I didn't have a perfect childhood, and that where you start isn't always where you end up. I hoped this would demonstrate that, no matter what challenges he faces in life, having faith in God can help turn things around if he continues to believe in the possibilities.

While I wanted him always to see me as his Superman, I realized I was a father doing everything I could to raise my son.

Chapter 24

Healing of the Heart

ednesday morning arrived brisk and gray.

A sudden cold front pressed down on the city, hinting at rain before the weekend. My coffee sat steadily in the cup holder, steam rising like a small comfort as I drove to work. It should have felt like an ordinary morning, quiet and predictable, but a low unease lingered beneath the surface, settling in my ribs without any clear explanation. I overlooked the missed calls until I pulled into my reserved space in the school parking lot. *Do Not Disturb* had done its job too well.

Several of my mother's notifications glared back at me.

Inside my office, I set my laptop bag down, finished the last swallow of coffee, and called her immediately.

"Hello, Mom. Is everything okay? I saw all the missed calls."

"I'm fine," she said quickly, then hesitated. "I just… I couldn't sleep. I've been thinking all night about your father. About not being honest with you."

I leaned back in my chair, choosing my words carefully. "Mom, I don't want this to sound harsh, but it wasn't exactly a mystery. When I showed you that picture, your face said everything. I'm a grown man now. Did you really think I couldn't handle the truth?"

She exhaled softly. "I saw the life you built, your career, your family, that beautiful home, and I thought maybe… maybe I had protected you well enough."

She paused, then added, timidly, "All those days I took you to the library, tried to keep you focused… I hoped they mattered."

They did, though I had never said it.

"Mom," I said quietly, "I need to be honest with you, too. And I need you to hear me."

"I'm listening."

For a moment, I searched for the right place to begin.

"I learned early how to keep things inside. I never wanted to feel like a burden to you. You were always working, always tired. And the older I got, the more I convinced myself that feeling anything at all was a weakness."

I swallowed.

"I love being a husband to Lisa. I love being Zion's father. But I'm constantly wondering if I'm doing it right. And now... finding out this truth has shaken something loose. How am I supposed to adjust to a man who was never there?"

Silence stretched between us.

"You told me my father was a war hero," I added, my voice lower now. "Not a criminal. That hurts, Mom. It feels like a betrayal."

"Son, that was a lifetime ago," she said gently.

"I know. But you taught me to value honesty. To be transparent. Can you see the contradiction?"

"What was I supposed to tell you? That your father was a manipulator? Violent? Everything I prayed you wouldn't become? His being gone was the best thing that could've happened for us. We struggled, but we survived."

"Yeah," I said, the words heavier now. "But you couldn't teach me how to be a man." I heard her inhale sharply.

"I know you tried to fill both roles," I continued, gentler but firm. "But some lessons must come from somewhere. I didn't learn how to shave, tie a tie, or balance a checkbook until much later, until Deacon Candors stepped in."

"That's what I thought Sledge would do," she said. "He promised he would take care of you. Of us."

"But he didn't take care of you," I said. The memory surfaced without warning.

At first, Sledge seemed kind. Protective. My mother wanted to believe that having a man in the house meant safety and stability. But insecurity crept in quickly, then control. Arguments over nothing. Accusations that made no sense. Doors slammed. Voices raised.

At the pool hall, men stared. Some flirted.

Sledge drank.

His temper followed us home.

I remembered the sound of glass shattering in the bedroom, picture frames crashing against the wall.

My mother's body hit the plaster.

I was eight.

I remembered the weight of the gun in my shaking hands, pulled from the lampstand drawer. The hallway felt impossibly narrow. My voice didn't sound like mine when I screamed for him to leave.

"This isn't over," he said, backing toward the door.

But it was.

I bolted the locks. I watched until his truck disappeared. My mother slid down the wall, blood at her mouth, one hand pressed to her ribs. She took the gun from me gently and pulled me into her arms until the shaking stopped.

"Mom," I said now, my voice unsteady, "that night never left me."

"I know," she whispered. "I didn't love myself then. If I had, I would have left sooner. But after that... I swore you would never see that again."

"I don't blame you," I said. "I just didn't realize how much it shaped me."

She was quiet for a moment.

"You turned out to be a good man, Jacob."

Those words captivated my heart. I felt something heal inside.

"I needed to say these things," I told her. "I wish it had been in person. But I'm glad we talked."

"I'm glad too," she said. "With everything happening in your life, don't forget how much you're loved."

"I won't, Mom."

152

Chapter 25

Reflection from a Distance

T he morning settled with a familiar calm.

I opened the blinds and let the gray light spill across the space of my office, pausing long enough to take in the quiet before reaching for my handheld radio.

My channel set.

Outside, students were already arriving, parents easing into the carline, the rhythm of routine grounding me before the day could scatter my thoughts.

I skimmed my inbox, adjusted the final details of that evening's faculty meeting agenda, and leaned into the comfort of small tasks, emails answered, signatures added, order restored. It was only when I lifted my head that I noticed him.

***

Richard stood just beyond the glass doors of the front office.

My pulse shifted. I hadn't given him my work address, hadn't carved out time, hadn't invited him into this part of my life. His posture was tense, his steps quick but uncertain, as if urgency had pushed him here despite hesitation. Whatever he carried with him hadn't waited for permission.

The intercom crackled.

"Mr. Foster, there's a guest at the front desk who says he knows you and has something important to share. Would you like me to send him in?" Mrs. Robinson asked.

I hesitated for only a moment. I had fifteen minutes, no more.

"Yes. Please send him in. Thank you."

I straightened the papers on my desk as she escorted him down the hall, a reflexive act of control.

"Come in, Richard," I said evenly, the tone I used when I needed to lead rather than feel. "Please, have a seat."

I asked Mrs. Robinson to hold my calls for the next twenty minutes, an unspoken boundary.

Richard took it in at once.

His eyes moved slowly around the room: the degrees lining the wall, the awards, the framed photograph of my family,

154

Lisa's smile frozen in sunlight, Zion perched on my shoulders, proof of a life built without him.

"You've done well for yourself," he said quietly. "This is… impressive."

"Thank you," I replied, already impatient. "What brings you here?"

"I wanted to tell you in person." His voice wavered. "I had my niece help me look you up. She found the school's website and read about your awards. National Principal of the Year. Twice." He shook his head in awe.

It felt like a preamble. I leaned against the desk, arms crossed.

"I can see you're busy," he said carefully. "Then let's get to it."

He inhaled. "I know how complicated your feelings are about your father, but I wanted you to understand his side."

"Amaze me," I replied flatly. Richard didn't flinch.

"Your father was wrongfully convicted of a crime he didn't commit. New forensic testing and technology that didn't exist back then have proven it. He was released yesterday after thirty-eight years."

The words landed heavily.

"He'll eventually receive compensation, but it could take

time. Until then, he's staying with me." Richard swallowed. "What grieves him most is knowing he lost every chance to know you."

I stood up straighter. "I'm glad justice was finally served, truly. But that doesn't change what my mother and I experienced. Those years didn't disappear just because the truth has surfaced late."

Silence stretched between us.

"What's done is done," I added, already wanting to end the conversation. "Thank you for coming."

Richard reached for the door.

"Wait," I said.

He turned, hope flickering in his expression despite himself.

"Where is he?"

Richard looked down.

"He's in the car. He didn't want to embarrass you or cause a scene at your workplace. He said he didn't feel... presentable."

I nodded in understanding.

"Tomorrow night at Market Center Boulevard. Eight o'clock at the Diner."

Richard's breath caught.

"He'll be there."

After he left, I stood at the window, watching the car pull away. The windshield reflected only the sky, cloudy, unreadable. I searched for a face I couldn't see.

Curiosity pressed against caution. Hope against old defenses.

I wasn't sure if meeting him would bring clarity or break something fragile within me, but the distance between us no longer felt safe enough to keep.

Chapter 26

Meeting at the Diner

Standing on the edge of a choice that could quietly change my life, I knew this meeting would either close a door I'd kept shut for decades or open it in ways I wasn't sure I could handle. The letter from my father sat folded in my jacket pocket, its words worn from rereading. His wish to reconnect stirred something unsettled inside me: resentment mixed with curiosity; anger intertwined with longing.

I carried my mother's struggles with me as I drove. The long nights. The quiet endurance. The way his absence had felt less like distance and more like erasure. Still, the unanswered questions pressed harder than the pain. I realized that avoiding him wouldn't protect me; it would only prolong the uncertainty. If I wanted clarity, this was the cost.

Rain fell lightly as I drove, a fine mist coating the windshield. I cracked the window, letting the cool air steady my breathing. I called Lisa before pulling up to the Diner, not to explain, but to anchor myself. She listened without interruption, then prayed, softly, deliberately, before we hung up. By the time I parked, I felt steadier, though no less guarded.

Before stepping out, I closed my eyes and whispered, "God, give me the strength to face what's coming. And the grace to forgive, if forgiveness is possible."

Inside, the Diner smelled of coffee and fried batter. I flipped the collar of my peacoat down and asked for a booth with a clear view of the entrance. I wanted to see him before he saw me. Control mattered tonight.

The waitress set the menus down. I asked for two more and water with lemon. Then I excused myself to the restroom, splashed cold water on my face, and stared at my reflection, searching for the boy I'd been, bracing the man I'd become. When I returned to the table, I began studying the menu as rain created trails, like veins of water, sliding down the window beside me.

When Richard walked in, my father was close behind. Keith looked older than I'd imagined. His tan jacket hung loosely on his frame. His beard was untrimmed but clean, his movements careful, measured. He walked with the stiffness of someone used to taking his steps carefully. When his eyes met mine, he slowed, not in hesitation, but in restraint.

His voice was quiet. Not tentative.

Contained.

"Hi," he said. "I'm Keith. I've been waiting for this moment."

His handshake was warm, slightly damp. He didn't hold on longer than necessary. Richard peeled away to another table without a word, leaving us to sit alone with the weight of the moment.

The waitress hovered, then gently said, "I'll give you a minute."

Keith nodded in thanks but didn't look away from me.

"I know this isn't easy," he said finally. "And I know there's no fixing what I broke. But I wanted to try."

"Try what?"

The words came out sharper than I intended. "Thirty-eight years passed without you in my life. What exactly are you trying to do now?"

He didn't interrupt. He didn't flinch.

"You missed everything," I continued, heat rising fast. "First days. First failures. Everything that made me who I am. I built my life without you. So, tell me, what do you think you can add to it now?"

My hands clenched under the table. My voice carried farther than I meant it to.

Keith stayed still, absorbing each word without defense.

"Jacob," he said gently, lifting one hand as if to steady the air between us. "I won't argue with your pain. You're right to be angry."

That almost made it worse.

"Do you think I didn't want to be there?" he continued. "I replay those years every day. I wasn't free. I wasn't innocent. I was surviving something I didn't understand yet. And I failed you anyway."

He swallowed, eyes steady.

"I'm not here to rewrite history."

The Diner had gone quiet. I felt eyes on us. The pressure mounted.

"I hurt your mother," he said.

"You're darn right you hurt my mother!" I started to boil inside. Fist quivering, heart began to race.

"I hurt you. I can see it. I will never forgive myself for it. Prison didn't change that; it just gave me time to see it clearly. I'm not asking you to be your father. I'm asking for forgiveness. If that's something you can ever give."

I stood before he finished speaking. Time felt suddenly dangerous.

"I need to go," I said, pulling out my wallet. I placed a hundred-dollar bill on the table. "Thank you for saying what you needed to say."

I met his eyes once more.

"I heard you."

Then I turned away before my resolve failed.

Outside, rain clung to my coat.

Through the Diner window, I saw Keith fold inward, his face buried in his hands. Richard sat beside him, quiet, present.

In my car, the questions came fast and mercilessly.

Had I come too soon?

Or had I waited too long?

Was that anger mine or the voice of the child who never got answers?

I started the engine but didn't pull away.

Somewhere beneath the confusion, something fragile stirred, not forgiveness, not yet, but the unsettling possibility that this wasn't the end.

It may be the beginning.

Chapter 27

The Long Way Home

My mind replayed fragments of the Diner conversation as I drove home in silence, no radio, just the rhythm of tires cutting through shallow puddles. I cracked the window, letting the cool air steady me, as if it might clear the noise; I couldn't shut myself off.

By the time I pulled into the driveway, the night had settled in. Crickets chirped, and frogs croaked from the lake beyond the backyard. Inside, the house was quiet. Lisa and Zion slept peacefully, unaware of the turmoil I was bringing back with me. I gently closed the door and stepped onto the patio, guided by the moonlight. I opened my phone and read about the importance of forgiving so that one can be forgiven. Those words felt heavier than rain.

The weight of the concept pressed down on me. I understood the principle, but I didn't grasp the cost.

Forgiveness felt like being asked to absorb a debt I hadn't created.

"God," I said quietly, careful not to wake anyone, "I need clarity. I don't know how to hold this without it hardening me."

I didn't raise my voice. I didn't bargain. I stayed there long enough to admit what I'd been avoiding, that the anger I aimed at Keith had roots deeper than him. Fear. Inadequacy. The quiet dread of becoming the very man I resented.

Rain began to fall, not suddenly, but steadily. I stepped beyond the patio cover and let it soak through me. I didn't cry out. I didn't collapse. I stood there, letting the moment do its work, until the tightness in my chest loosened.

I wasn't better than him. I was just earlier in the story.

When I stepped back under the patio, drenched and calmer, the answer felt simple, not easy, but clear.

Mercy wasn't excusing what happened. It was choosing not to let it keep happening inside me.

I called Richard immediately, not wanting the moment to pass unused.

"Hello?" His voice was thick with sleep.

"Richard, I'm sorry to call so late. I need to speak with

Keith. Is he there?"

"He was about fifteen minutes ago but left to go on a walk. He does that when his head gets heavy. Is everything alright?"

"I owe him an apology," I said. "And I owe you one too."

"You don't owe me anything," Richard replied. "But Keith… he took it hard. He meant what he said tonight. He wasn't posturing. He was trying."

"Please tell him I called," I said. "Tell him I'm sorry, and that I meant what I said about listening."

"I will."

I hesitated, then added, "We're having Family Day at church this Sunday. If you're willing, I'd like him to come. With you."

There was a pause, then warmth in Richard's voice.

"He'd appreciate that more than you know." "Thank you."

When I ended the call, the house was still quiet. The rain had slowed. I went inside, changed my clothes, and checked on Lisa and Zion one more time before turning in.

Chapter 28

Family Day

Blue skies stretched overhead, the sun radiant but gentle, as if creation itself had agreed to cooperate. It was the kind of day that made forgiveness feel possible, even if it wasn't yet complete.

Family and Friends Day had drawn a whole house. Ralph and India were our guests, and while I smiled and greeted people as we made our way inside, my eyes kept drifting toward the entrance. I hoped Keith would come. I needed him to come, not to fix everything, but to prove that last night hadn't been wasted grace.

After dropping Zion off at Children's Ministry, we entered

the lobby, which buzzed with activity. Latecomers grabbing coffee, parents rushing kids upstairs, the bookstore crowded with last-minute purchases. I scanned every familiar face.

Nothing.

As the praise team finished their opening song, I stepped back into the foyer, searching again, still no sign of him.

"Don't worry, babe," Lisa whispered when I returned. "I'm sure there's a good reason he's running late."

I nodded, though my chest remained tight.

Visitors were welcomed from the stage, the room alive with warmth and conversation. I tried to focus, but my thoughts kept circling back to the empty seat I'd imagined Keith occupying.

"Just so you know," India whispered, leaning in, "if they ask me to say anything, I'm pleading the blood and sitting down immediately."

Ralph didn't look at her. "You'll be fine," he said quietly. "Just… don't volunteer."

"That's discriminatory," India muttered.

Lisa leaned over before it could escalate. "India," she said evenly, not scolding, "we're glad you're here. Just sit with us, okay?"

India studied her for a beat, then nodded. "Fair."

"The Lord knows my heart!" she declared, raising a hand heavenward. "Y'all just pray for me."

Lisa kept a watchful eye on her as the choir began to sing.

Their voices washed over the sanctuary, full, warm,

healing. The song carried the same theme that had undone me in the rain days earlier. Forgiveness. Release. Redemption.

Dr. Moore's message felt uncomfortably precise, as if God had handed him my journal. With every word, something inside me loosened. By the time he extended the altar call for those struggling to let go. I was already standing. I knelt at the steps of the platform. Ralph stood nearby. The music swelled, and suddenly a hand rested on my shoulder.

"Jacob... "

I looked up through tears. Keith stood before me.

"I'm so sorry," he said, his voice breaking.

He stood there, unsure whether he had the right to touch me.

"No," I said, pulling him into an embrace. "I need your forgiveness."

We clung to each other as Ralph handed us tissues and a church leader joined us in prayer. I felt lighter than I had in years, not because the past was erased, but because it no longer owned me.

After service, I introduced Keith to Lisa, India, and Ralph.

"I hear you have a son," Keith said, smiling softly. "I do," I replied. "We need to pick him up."

Lisa touched my arm gently. "Before we bring Zion back, can we pause for a second?" I nodded.

"I want to support this," she said carefully. "I do. But I also need us to agree on how we introduce him to your father, not just that we do."

"What do you mean?"

"Zion doesn't have context," she said. "And Keith is still finding his footing. I'm not saying no. I'm asking for intention."

I exhaled, the edge leaving me. "You're not afraid of him."

"No," she said. "I'm protective of all of you." When I rejoined Keith and Ralph, Keith's expression told me he already understood.

Keith glanced toward the hallway once, then back at me.

"I think I'll step out," he said calmly. "This is a lot for one morning."

"You don't have to…"

I know," he said. "But I don't want to be the reason for tension in your home. Not again."

Richard arrived soon after, and Keith left quietly.

Chapter 29

Reflection

After church, I ironed Zion's school uniform and prepared his lunch for the next day. The steady rhythm of my routine helped quiet my thoughts after such an emotionally charged day. While I worked, Lisa called India to thank her for joining us at church and for always being there when things got complicated.

Before turning in for the night, I felt compelled to call my mother. It wasn't just to check on her; it was also a moment of reflection. I needed to examine my own behavior, acknowledge where I might have fallen short, and share what had happened that day.

The phone rang twice before she answered. In that brief pause, I realized how often growth begins with uncomfortable conversations.

"Hello," my mother said.

"Hey, Mother. Are you busy?" I asked.

"No, I'm just sitting here watching television… or rather, the television is watching me," she replied, amusement softening her voice.

"I've got some good news," I said. "What's that?" she asked, alert. I heard the television volume lower, the faint crackle fading into silence as anticipation filled the space between us.

"You'll never guess who came to church today." "Who?"

"Keith."

There was a pause.

"You don't say," she replied slowly. "Richard told me he was out and had been looking for you. How did he find you so fast?"

"Richard coordinated everything," I said.

I walked her through everything: how Richard and I crossed paths, how the pieces fell together, and how that chance meeting led us to the Diner. I didn't hold back on the details, the anger, the pain, and the moment I had to confront emotions I thought I had buried long ago. As I recounted inviting Keith to church, I imagined my mother growing quietly on the other end of the line, retreating inward and bracing herself against memories she had tried to silence for years.

"Wait a minute," she said sharply. "I thought you didn't want to know who he was after what he did to me, especially after how upset you were the other night. Now you're defending him. Whose side are you on?"

The question hit me harder than I expected. Whose side was I on?

For a moment, I didn't answer. Then I realized this wasn't about choosing sides; it was about choosing truth.

"The side of truth, Mom," I said carefully. "Wasn't it you who told me I should forgive him? Should I go back to treating him like dirt? Everyone deserves a second chance."

"That may be true," she replied, disappointment heavy in her voice, "but it amazes me how quickly you seem willing to give him a pass. Like nothing ever happened."

"I'm not saying what he did was okay," I said.

"When I first saw him, I was seconds away from punching him and ruining my own life in the process. I was that angry. But something stopped me."

I paused. "There are still triggers, especially with him. But someone must be the bigger person. If I learned anything from you, it was that."

Then I added, "And honestly, Mom… when I confronted him, I didn't find the monster I expected. I found a broken man. Lost. Weak. Afraid. He looked like someone who had already lost everything. Hitting him didn't feel worth my peace."

"Serves him right," she huffed. "He finally got what he deserved."

"That's harsh, Mom. Do you feel that way after all these years?"

"If you were me, you'd understand," she said bitterly. "I've always put everyone else first."

Her words carried years of quiet resentment… sacrifices layered upon sacrifices, never released, only buried.

She had stayed late at work so I could go on field trips, given up nights out, and new clothes to pay for school supplies. And through it all, she kept her own pain tucked away so no one else would have to carry it.

I realized then that forgiveness looked different for her, and forcing it would only deepen the wound.

"I'm praying for you, Mom," I said gently. "And for myself too. How have you been feeling lately? I've been worried about you."

She sighed. "My legs and feet have been sore. Tingling sometimes. Poor circulation, I think. I bought compression socks, but they only help a little."

"Are you taking your blood pressure medication?"
"Not lately."

"Mom," I said carefully, keeping my tone soft, "we can come up with a plan together to help you remember. I know it's not easy, but I want to support you."

"I know, son."

"Knowing and doing aren't the same."

She chuckled. "Did you call to talk about your father or my health?"

"Both," I said. "You matter too."

"I'm fine," she said. "How's my grandson?"

"He's doing well," I replied.

Her question reminded me of something I had been meaning to ask. "Mom… could you come by tomorrow for a couple of hours? Lisa and I would like to spend some intentional time together. Things have felt a little heavier lately. We just need a little support." "Say no more," she said. "I'll come by. I can bake those cookies I promised Zion… and a carrot cake for you."

I smiled, feeling the tension ease from my shoulders.

"You're amazing."

"I'll be over tomorrow evening. Does that work?"

"Perfect."

"Alright then. I love you."

"I love you too, Mom. And please… don't forget your meds."

"Who's the parent here?" she teased.

"You are," I laughed. "I'm just reminding you."

"Nothing's happened to me yet," she said proudly.

"Exactly," I replied.

We said our goodbyes, and when the line went silent, I sat quietly for a moment.

Chapter by chapter, conversation by conversation, I was learning that forgiveness wasn't just a single act; it was a process. One that required patience, courage, and the willingness to face discomfort head-on.

And tomorrow would bring a little more healing.

Chapter 30

Love Deposit

Mother arrived with groceries in hand and a story already halfway told.

The new gate guard didn't recognize her and subjected her to a thorough interrogation.

Mother leaned in, smiled knowingly, and said, "If you've got a bone to pick, just wait until my son asks for my soul food. You'll wish you'd let me through sooner." She laughed all the way up the driveway, shaking her head as if she had won a small but satisfying victory.

Inside, she unloaded ingredients for a complete meal: greens, seasonings, and things she claimed real people ate. Mother called our place the "rabbit house," insisting that our refrigerator was stocked exclusively with lettuce and carrots.

Her playful jabs at Lisa about being too skinny to keep a husband warm in winter were layered with affection she often struggled to express. Once, I'd told her what Lisa had cooked for dinner.

"Son," she said bluntly, "that's not dinner. You'd be better off buying bird feed." Lisa had overheard and shot back, smiling, "At least the birds would eat like royalty." That was how they loved each other, through laughter, sarcasm, and small, honest moments.

***

When I got home from work that evening, I took a hot shower and changed into linen pants and a white shirt, the cool fabric comforting against my skin. The anticipation of the night ahead buzzed beneath the surface.

Upstairs, Lisa moved softly, her footsteps light with excitement. I packed her favorite throw blanket, loaded the picnic basket with fruit, candles, and sparkling cider, and paused once everything was in the car, feeling grounded and grateful. Not long ago, I wouldn't have slowed down enough to notice how much this moment mattered.

"Babe," I called, standing in the foyer. "You ready?"

"Just a minute," she answered.

Then she appeared. Lisa descended the stairs in a deep-V bohemian maxi dress, the fabric swaying with each step. The slit revealed just enough legs to stop me in my tracks. I forgot how to breathe.

"Wow," was all I managed to say. She laughed, blushing.

"You like it?"

"Like it?" I crossed the room, spinning her gently.

"I love it. Are you sure you're my wife?"

She laughed harder as I snapped a picture on my phone. I caught a flicker in her eyes: vulnerability, pride, relief, and my chest tightened.

"Jacob," she said, smiling, "we have to go."

"Mom's in the kitchen with Zion," I teased. "This house is huge. She'll never know."

She kissed me quickly, laughing. "Do you ever turn off Mr. Energizer Bunny?"

I called out to my mother as we headed for the door, but Zion beat us there.

"Where are you going?" he asked, eyes wide.

"To take your mother on a date," I replied.

"Mom," he said, impressed. "You look like a model."

"That's because she is," I said, nudging him aside. "Now kiss your mother so we can go." He did and hugged me, finally allowing us to escape.

As I started the car, Lisa placed her hand on my knee.

"Wait," she said softly. "I have a secret." She leaned in, fingers brushing my arm, her voice low and teasing. I nearly stalled the engine.

"Babe," I laughed nervously, pulling out of the driveway, "If we don't leave right now, this night is going to end early."

Lisa laughed as we drove toward the blues and jazz festival, the tension between us warm, playful, and alive.

***

At the park, I laid out the blanket on a small hill overlooking the lights and music. Candles flickered softly, casting intimate shadows. "This is beautiful," Lisa whispered. I wiped a tear from the corner of her eye. "Did you know I'd cry?" she asked. "No," I said honestly. "But I hoped it might mean something." She took my hand. "It does." The music drifted through the air as we lay side by side, talking not about logistics or stress or schedules, but about us, about fears we hadn't voiced, about promises we needed to keep.

"I don't want us to lose each other," she said.

"We won't," I replied. "Not if we keep choosing this."

Chapter 31

M other answered the phone.
"Hello."

"Good morning, Mom. I wanted to thank you again for helping us last night. We had a chance to rekindle the fire again."

"No problem."

"Mom, I forgot to tell you, you left your medication last night in a small paper bag. Did you need it? I'm sure I can drop it off."

"I'm ok, just drop it off after you get off work." Her voice had a tired undertone as it crackled through the phone. I could almost hear the faint rattle of the pill bottle and feel the crumpled paper bag in my hands. "What medicine is it? Your high-blood pressure medication and inhaler?"

"I will be ok," she said sleepily.

"Do you at least have an extra inhaler?"

"I'm sure it's in the medicine cabinet somewhere. I should be fine, especially since guess who's coming to see me?"

She changed the subject, which she always does when discussing her health. Her reluctance to address these issues used to frustrate me, but over time, I realized it was her way of staying in control, not wanting to burden anyone with her struggles. Yet, this tendency worried me, making me question if there was more she wasn't telling.

"Is it Mrs. Baker, the widow who walks in the neighborhood every day?"

"Good guess, but no. It's Keith. He wants to stop by. Says he's a new man since Sunday at church. I'm not sure; it feels like an excuse to see me. That's not the Keith I know," she said, followed by a slight pause.

A faint cough punctuated her words, making me briefly worried about her breathlessness. But, just as quickly, she moved on, brushing any concern aside.

"He told me he was trying to get his life together when we spoke after the service. I never thought I would say this, but something tells me he means it." I said.

"Well, I'll believe it when I see it," she replied, not fully convinced. "I thought he was crazy calling me on Sunday afternoon from Richard's phone, apologizing for all the horrible things he did and said in the past. Like he'd lost his marbles."

"He did have a lot of time to think about things in prison. Time to reflect on what was important in life. I guess we finally made his list."

"We'll see, I reckon." She spoke.

"Let me know how it goes. I must go, but I love you, Mom."

"I love you too, son. See you soon."

I wondered if my father had already stopped by. If he had, what was the topic of the conversation they were having? Were they discussing the possibility of getting back together after all these years? Did he have more kids she didn't know about that could be my half-brothers and sisters? All kinds of thoughts ran through my mind during leadership meetings, as I walked the hallways, checked on classrooms, and spoke to high schoolers along the way.

My phone buzzed with a notification: a missed call from an unknown number, and my heart skipped a beat. I couldn't help but fear it was related to something urgent with my mom, adding another layer of anxiety to the already chaotic day.

Feeling as if I had walked the length of a marathon, I re-tied to the office to respond to emails while resting my legs. My cell phone rang fifteen minutes later with shocking news.

"Jacob! Are you able to leave right now? Your mother is having trouble breathing. I've called 911, and the ambulance is on its way!"

"What?" I stood up, causing my office chair to shoot from under me.

"Get here fast, she's hyperventilating!"

"Ok, keep my mom's phone with you so I can call you. I'm leaving now!" I grabbed my keys on my way to the car, and I told my secretary to let the vice-principal know I needed to leave due to an emergency.

I drove to my mother's house as fast as traffic would allow. Then, a construction zone halted me, a roadblock reminding me of the unresolved issues between us, years of unspoken words and silent pleas for peace. My heart was pounding. I turned on the hazard lights. Each second stretched, like reliving moments of past helplessness. I felt powerless and desperate. Praying for a miracle, like Moses parting the Red Sea.

Keith called me just as I made a left turn onto her street, urging me to head to the hospital instead. Feeling relieved, he was with her in the back of the ambulance, and they passed by me in a flash, sirens and lights whirling. The ambulance shot past on my left, weaving through the traffic as if parting a sea. I slammed my vehicle into reverse in the middle of the road to turn around and follow, which accidentally ended the call. As I fumbled with my phone for an update, it slipped through my fingers and fell between the seat's crack beyond my reach. I heard my father's voice with distant chatter. I answered loudly, hoping he could hear me tell him to wait while I switched the call to the vehicle phone.

As I repeatedly pressed the recall button on the car display, it kept going to my mother's voicemail. I wished she had listened to me, constantly telling her to keep her cell phone charged for unexpected cases like this, but her stubbornness would always triumph.

Finally, I arrived in time to see her pulled from the ambulance. Throwing open the car door, I ran as fast as I could to try to talk to her and see if she was okay. I noticed the mist of her oxygen mask and her pale skin with the rise and fall of her chest as she struggled with breathing.

"Please step back, sir," the EMT said in a hurried tone as the wheels of the stretcher rapidly unfolded, hitting the ground.

Everything was happening at quantum speed, yet I stood there in slow-motion, like a scene from the Matrix. My father held her hand until they wheeled her through the sliding doors of the Emergency Room. For a moment, the world fell silent. The urgency of the situation washed over me in that brief pause. The chaos around seemed to hush, amplifying the gravity of the moment.

"Go! Park the car and come inside," Keith said to me, snapping me out of the haze before rushing to be with my mother as they rushed her to an area to begin working on her.

It took what it seemed like forever to find a parking space and run back inside to see how she was. I asked to go see her once inside but was told it was better to wait in the waiting area because the doctor would be out at any moment.

I paced the floor of the waiting room, sitting down only to try to calm my nerves while checking my watch every five to ten seconds. The doctor and my father came from inside the Emergency room to get me so I could see her. I did my best not to think the worst, though my doubts were banging on faith's door.

I followed them through the cold hallway, hearing our heels clicking as we walked, before he introduced himself and told me what had happened.

"Mr. Jacob, my name is Dr. Lum. It's a good thing your father called 911 when he did." He paused, allowing the gravity of the situation to sink in. "A few minutes more and your mother would not be with us," he added gently, waiting for my response.

The room felt tense as I processed what he was saying.

"What happened?" I said, concerned.

Dr. Lum took a quiet breath, his clipboard pressed against his chest. He looked directly at me, and for a moment, the room felt suspended in time. "Your mother... " he paused, letting the weight sit between us, "had a heart attack." Silence filled the space, his gaze steady on mine, giving the words room to settle. "The good news is we were able to stabilize her." He waited again, watching for my reaction, before continuing gently, "We would like to keep her overnight to run further tests and see if she needs a pacemaker due to her slow heartbeat."

"Can I see her now?" I said nervously.

"Of course. Right this way," he said as we continued a few steps more to the sliding curtains where my mother lay still with her eyes closed.

"Hey Mom," I whispered, taking her soft hand in mine. My father came and stood beside me, not saying a word. I did not want to let her see me cry if she opened her eyes. She always told me I needed to be strong. I was certainly trying, but my heart was too heavy.

And as if my father could read my thoughts, he said, "You don't have to be strong. It's ok, I'm here."

I leaned over her body and wept because I thought I had lost her forever. Every breath she took, though faint, gave me hope for her recovery.

***

I took a couple of days off to ensure my mother was ok, while my assistant Principal took charge of my daily responsibilities. I felt a sense of solace, being there just in case she needed anything.

Carefully, I reached over and brushed a wisp of hair from her forehead. Her hair felt soft and fine, cool to my touch, and I smoothed the strands away from her temple.

She tried to pull off her oxygen mask, her fingers trembling, but I gently wrapped my hand around hers, my thumb tracing the curve of her knuckles, and gave the softest squeeze, letting her know it was all right to leave the mask on.

We stayed like that for a moment, her hand nested in mine, our fingers twined together. In the hush of the hospital room, these small acts, brushing her hair back, holding her hand, sharing the silent company, became their own language. Through them, I hoped she felt my presence, that unspoken promise that I would not let her face this alone.

"Mom, try not to move too much. You'll need all the energy and oxygen you can get right now." My voice trembled slightly despite my calm exterior at the sight of her vulnerability and the ache in my chest. As I stood there, a blend of relief and an overwhelming sense of protectiveness washed over me.

"You have no idea how much I count on being there for your mother as a privilege. It was an act of God. I'm thankful He chose me," Keith said.

My heart softened at that moment, and my view of him changed even more. It was as if God was showing me his heart in a way I had never seen before, and I let go of my hate against him. I saw him lovingly interacting with my mother as if he had not missed a day since I was born, and it was special.

At that moment, I realized that my feelings towards him had shifted. I no longer saw him as the man who had hurt my mother, but as a caring individual who had been there for her when she needed him the most. It was a profound moment of emotional healing and growth for me.

"Jacob, I can see that she's stable, so it's okay for you to leave if you need to. I promise to take loving care of her. I've already lost her once; I can't bear the thought of losing her again." He looked at my mother with such kindness in his eyes.

"I'll be okay here with her. But thanks!"

I called Lisa to let her know what happened and asked her to arrange for India to pick up Zion from school, since she had an important meeting with an overseas client that evening.

Lisa later texted me that Zion wanted me to call him before bed because it wasn't normal for me not to be home when he'd expected me. Lisa had not yet revealed the news to him, thinking it was best to come from me.

I stepped out into the hallway while Keith remained in the hospital room.

"Hi, Dad!" Zion said.

"Hey, buddy. I miss you!"

"I miss you too! Are you ok?"

"I'm fine, son." My heart was filled with warmth at his genuine concern for me.

"Where are you?" Zion said, hearing the worry in his voice, made me wish I could reach through the phone to hug him.

"I'm at the hospital."

"Are you hurt, Dad?"

"No son. I'm with Grandma Ella."

"What happened to Grandma Ella?" I could hear the fear in his voice and tried to reassure him as much as I could.

"I'm with her because she is not feeling well, but she is going to be okay."

"Daddy, should we pray?"

"Of course, we should. Would you like to lead the prayer?"

"Yes, sir. God, bless Grandma Ella to get well, and Daddy, if he's sad, make him happy again. Thank You for Mommy and her love for us, and Lord, please watch over Aunt India and Uncle Ralph so they can get married one day, because it's been a long time and they fight a lot! In Jesus Name Amen!"

"Amen!" Lisa and I chuckled.

"Good night, Daddy."

"Good night, son. I love you!"

"I love you too, Daddy!"

"Pass the phone to your mother, okay? Get some sleep."

"I will," Zion waved, and in a flash, he was gone.

"Zion, don't go to bed without brushing your teeth!" Lisa's voice echoed.

"Zion says the most random things! I sure needed that laugh," I said, chuckling.

"He's definitely your son!" Lisa smiled.

"So, I guess it's safe to say you two are doing alright?" I asked.

"More than okay. Although Zion's passing gas in the car is something else! It must have been those beans the school cafeteria served with the tacos, rice, and chocolate milk."

"Yeah, that will definitely do it," I laughed.

"So, how are you doing? Any news or updates on Grandma Ella?"

"Not yet, but then again, I only arrived about ten minutes ago," I replied.

Just as I finished speaking, Dr. Lum walked around the corner on his way to my mother's room.

"Babe, let me call you right back. I want to hear what the doctor has to say, okay? I love you."

"I will be praying for both of you," Lisa said before ending the video call.

I entered the room to find my mother and father engaged in a light conversation. I could hear occasional coughs and her request for a sip of water.

"So, Doc, what's the latest update?" I asked, standing with my arms crossed while my father leaned on the bed's railing close to the window.

Dr. Lum explained, adjusting his glasses, "Well, after reviewing her medical history and blood work, we performed an MRI and a CT scan. We discovered that your mother's condition is called atrial fibrillation." He paused for a moment, searching for the right words. "Think of the heart like a drummer trying to keep tempo for a band. With atrial fibrillation, it's as if the drummer keeps missing the rhythm, sometimes speeding up, sometimes slowing down, never settling into a steady beat. This irregular pulse confuses the rest of the body, making it hard for everything to work together smoothly."

My father and I stood in stunned silence. Just then, the memory of an afternoon vividly flashed before me.

My mother was out shopping with me at a local mall. As we slowly climbed the stairs, I noticed her gripping the railing tighter with each step. Her breath had grown shallow, and beads of sweat trickled down her forehead. Halfway through, she paused, her face a mix of determination and discomfort.

"Just a minute," she had murmured, forcing a brave smile my way while clutching her chest lightly. It was only later that I realized those signs of fatigue and her complaints of shortness of breath during everyday tasks might have been more serious than any of us knew.

Sensing our confusion, Dr. Lum continued to inform us about the symptoms my mother experienced.

"You all are talking as if I'm dead or not even here," my mother chimed in as we stood near her bedside in a semi-huddle formation.

"Oh, Mother, I'm sorry. I just wanted to know what was going on and how I could help," I replied.

"And so do I! You know, it IS my body we're talking about," my mother said, hinting for us to close, to give way to her input as always.

"We understand your frustration, Ella," my father replied.

"Ah, what do you know? You just got out of prison, and now you're acting like you've been here the whole time?" my mother shot back, while Dr. Lum shifted uncomfortably, whistling as he looked around the room.

"Ms. Foster, there are treatments we can consider," he interrupted their heated exchange.

"Such as, Doctor?" Mom replied.

"We can administer medication to control your heart's rhythm or blood-thinning meds to prevent blood clots and reduce the chance of stroke. You could couple that with a more natural means, such as dieting and exercise. The worst-case scenario is surgery."

"Thank you, Doctor," I said.

"No problem. Well, Ms. Foster, if you need anything, be sure to give us a buzz," he said, his departure leaving us to grapple with the weight of the options he presented.

"So, Mom, what do you think?"

"I don't want the surgery. If I have a phobia of needles, you think I'm going to opt for surgery?"

"Mom, I'm worried about you. You know, from now on, you must cut back on all that soul food you cook. I know it's hard, but this is your life we are talking about," I said, my concern clear in my voice.

Mother sat in silence, her gaze shifting from one medical monitor to another as the gravity of the situation sank in.

"I guess you are right, because I don't like being in this place at all."

"I will talk to the doctor to see if we can get you referred to a specialist as soon as possible," I said.

She relaxed as we talked. I stayed with her until she had finished her meal and dozed off.

Chapter 32

The time was right for a man-to-man talk with my father, once my mother was sound asleep and the initial shock had passed.

We stepped outside the hospital, the cool night air providing a brief respite from the tension inside. Taking in sight of cars, passing by, I asked my father, "Why now? What are your intentions of being in her life again? Are you here to try to rebuild what was lost?" I said, standing to face him. He held my gaze steadily; sincerity reflected in his eyes.

"I never stopped loving your mother," he admitted, his

voice softening. "I was young and foolish then, not knowing how to love myself, let alone someone else. I let my jealousy and my brokenness take control. But I've changed since then. I am 62 years old now, and life is too short to be living with regret."

"You're really trying, huh *ol'* man?"

"With all that I have! I know I don't have much, but I've gained so much more. The only two people missing from my life are you and Ella. I just want a second chance; that's all I'm asking," he pleaded, his determination apparent.

"I appreciate your willingness to try, but I want you to understand that making those changes will take time."

***

The next morning, Keith walked into the room carrying flowers, while I sat in a chair beside my mother's bedside, chatting with her and watching him come in.

"I don't mean to interrupt, but I just wanted to see how you were doing?" Keith said softly to my mother as he came closer.

My mother turned her head with care, mindful of the tubes and wires that followed her movement.

She reached slightly toward the flowers, and I gently motioned for him to place them on the stand beside her.

She said nothing.

It was not the silence of anger, but of preservation, the kind that guards what little strength remains and keeps old pain where it belongs.

"I know this may not be the right time," Keith continued. "But I've had a lot of time to think since I've been out. And with you being here, I thought… I should try to make things as right as I can."

He set the flowers down carefully.

"I've got to go now." He said, turning to leave.

The room filled with the weight of what was left unsaid. I felt my mother's heart, the quiet ache in the way her hand rested on the bedsheet.

Watching Keith leave, I felt a swirl of emotions: relief that his visit was brief, sadness for the distance that still lingered between them, and a tense hope that perhaps some wounds could still be healed.

The heaviness in the room pressed on me. Deep down, I wished I could bridge the silence, say something to ease what neither of them could express.

My mother's hand rested softly on the sheet, carrying an ache too deep for words.

Unresolved.

Tension.

Even the faint scent of the discounted flowers, petals already loosening, felt like an echo of the past, neither of them was ready to revisit.

Chapter 33

Home is Where the Heart Is

The day had unfolded as expected. My heart lagged, tangled in its own confusion, trying to make sense of this new concept of a fragmented family among my mother, Keith, and me.

The drive home was quiet, the world outside blurring past as if I were gliding on autopilot. My mind sifted through a jumble of memories and moments, all crowding together in this strange, unsettled season of life.

It reminded me of an old sweater I had when I was a boy.

"Don't pull on that string, Jacob."

"What will happen if I do?"

"It will unravel." My mother would say.

Even as a boy, I clung to the belief that I could keep everything together. So, I kept tugging at that string, convinced I could mend the unraveling, only to watch the hole widen. That memory echoed as I walked through my front door that afternoon. The same stubborn hope whispering that if I just held on tight enough, everything would somehow stay intact.

***

Lisa found me adrift in my office chair, slowly spinning as I stared past the open Bible on my desk. She slipped in, wrapped me in a quiet hug, and disappeared upstairs to change, thinking I was lost in study rather than in thought. Zion stayed in his room, working on his science project as best he could, with Lisa stopping to help.

As time passed, Lisa and Zion trickled downstairs. Zion appeared at the office doorway, expectations written all over his face.

"Dad, where is dinner?"

"Oh..." I smiled faintly and glanced at my watch.

"Looks like I am running a little behind, son. I will be there in a minute."

"I'd ask Mom, but she just helped me with my homework. The real reason... " Zion leaned and whispered, "She always makes us eat healthy."

"And what do I do that's different from your mother?"

"You put seasoning on it."

We both laughed as quietly as possible.

"I heard that!" Lisa exclaimed from the front of the room.

"Your mother has supersonic hearing, you know. I'll be there in a minute."

"Ok, Dad."

In that moment, I sensed God working through my son, as He so often did, pulling me back from the edge of myself. Still, I wondered how long that rescue would last.

The Dinner Table

We lingered at the table, trading stories as the soft music of clinking silverware mingled with the rich scent of Tuscan Garlic Salmon, sun-dried tomatoes, wilted spinach, and

Zion's cherished Jiffy cornbread.

When I shared my childhood love for Jiffy cornbread, Zion insisted on tasting it and now pairs it with every meal, a quirky tradition just for us. Lisa, meanwhile, claims it tastes like sweetened sandpaper.

As the meal ended, Lisa's eyes sharpened, catching the subtle signs: my gaze drifting, my words clipped and sparse, my pauses stretching longer each time she asked about my day.

I let Zion's jokes carry on with the conversation, grateful for his easy laughter, even as I saw the worry building in Lisa's eyes. I knew a reckoning between us was only a matter of time.

The Bedroom

After dinner, with the kitchen gleaming and the dishwasher humming its gentle tune, we drifted to our rooms. Lisa's silence followed me, thick and unyielding, from the table through every nightly routine.

The chill of the sheets hinted at the difficult conversation I expected, but silence prevailed. Darkness settled, and I drifted toward sleep until a sudden flicker of the lamp, a cold rush as the covers shifted, and a gentle tap on my shoulder pulled me back.

"Jacob, we need to talk."

"Huh?" My pupils struggle to adjust to the light.

"We need to talk," Lisa repeated, gingerly shaking my shoulder again.

"About?"

"What's going on with you? I know you are not okay.

I want to know why you haven't been yourself lately."

"We have to talk about this now?"

I moaned, exhausted.

"Yes. I tried to allow you time to let me know what is going on with you, but as always, you hold it in. I want to know why."

"I'm good, babe." I pulled the covers up. "And besides, it's late."

A heavy hush settled between us.

Not heavy.

Full of things neither of us had named.

Lisa didn't rush.

She never did.

But when something felt off, she didn't let it drift either.

I stared at the ceiling, trying to outrun the feeling in my chest. Vulnerability had always felt foreign to me.

I knew how to lead.

Provide.

Stand firm.

But opening up?

That felt like stepping out without armor.

Growing up, strength meant absorbing pain and saying nothing. Speaking it aloud felt like breaking some unspoken code.

"I see you, Jacob," she said softly. "Don't you know

that? I didn't marry you just for your strength. I married you for your heart."

I swallowed but said nothing.

"It's not that I can't be vulnerable with you," I finally said. "I just… I need to process things first. Make sense of them before I start talking."

"Why do you have to do that alone?" she asked. I exhaled slowly. "Because it's a lot."

"Then let it be a lot with me."

Her words landed deeper than I expected.

"It's my mom," I said. "Seeing her like that. And my dad… I barely know him. One minute I'm trying to understand him, the next I'm questioning if I let him back in too quickly. I don't even know if he'll stay."

I paused.

"And Zion. How do I explain any of this to him when I don't even understand it myself?"

Lisa reached for my hand under the covers.

You don't have to have the answers tonight," she said. "And you don't have to carry all of this like it's a leadership role."

I gave a faint, tired smile. "That's how I'm wired." "I know," she replied gently. "But this isn't a job,

Jacob. It's your *heart*."

That one sat heavily. "I'm trying," I admitted.

"I know you are," she said. "But trying doesn't mean doing it alone."

Silence returned, but it felt different now.

Lisa leaned into me, wrapping her arms around my waist, resting her head against my chest. She didn't press for more words. She just stayed there.

And slowly, the weight of perfection I had carried for so long began to loosen its grip.

Chapter 34

The next day, I felt noticeably better, lighter, as if a soothing warmth had entered my body, loosening the tension in my shoulders.

My steps felt unhurried, in sync with a deep, calm breath that escaped my lips. Things felt more normal this time around. The weight I'd been carrying had loosened its grip, and even though, from a school principal's point of view, school wasn't picture-perfect, the day slowed just enough for me to find my rhythm again.

It was Lisa's turn to pick up Zion after school that evening, and with no plans, I found myself drawn to take an alternate route home.

There was something about the day that spoke to an

unspoken need within me, a quiet urge to reflect, to rediscover. As I turned onto an unfamiliar street, I realized I was headed towards my favorite place to breathe, *Barnes and Noble*, a haven where I hoped to find a moment's peace or a revelation amidst the bookshelves.

When I was a child, my mother used to take me to the library, encouraging me to check out books that would stretch my imagination. I remember one sun-drenched afternoon, the gentle dust motes dancing in a beam of sunlight as I sat on the floor, captivated by the adventures contained within the picture book in my hands. Those quiet hours spent wandering the aisles beside her remain some of my most cherished memories, simple moments of connection and discovery.

Even now, standing among shelves of stories fills me with the same sense of belonging and comfort, a return to the warmth I felt as a boy discovering new worlds one page at a time.

As I stepped inside the bookstore, a familiar calm settled over me. The scent of coffee lingered in the air, and there was comfort in being surrounded by strangers who shared the same quiet devotion, a kind of unspoken fellowship once reserved for bookworms. In a world dominated by glowing screens, places like this felt sacred: a refuge, a reminder of the pleasure and community found in printed words.

I moved through the store as if wandering through an art

museum, each book cover design a minor masterpiece. I lingered near sections on leadership, biblical history, and leather-bound vintage journals. The journals called out to me, a silent mirror for my state of mind, meant for ink-stained fingers and thoughtful pauses. They could be like a relic from another time, the kind that might have belonged in the hands of Jane Eyre or Charles Dickens, yet also connected with my own inner longing.

For the first time in days, my thoughts were not racing ahead or dragging me back.

I was present.

Drawn to a book about forgiveness and fatherhood, I was unsure which one to choose. I pulled them both off the shelf to look over instead and carried them to a two-person table near the coffee shop for easy access to my order when my name was called. The clatter of cups and the low murmur of conversation from the queue created a rhythm that foreshadowed something unexpected, a crescendo building under the hum of voices and the hiss of the coffee machine.

Placing the books on the small table to signal it was occupied, I stood behind a line of three customers, a few others joining behind me as I focused on the menu ahead.

I took my seat after ordering a black coffee with a few shots of espresso. I waited patiently for my name to be called as I browsed the covers and topics of both books.

"Jacob." The barista called.

I stood and walked to the counter to place my coffee order, noticing a young lady with a strikingly confident yet gentle gaze who followed me with her eyes as I sat at the table. Understanding that people were waiting behind her, she proceeded with her order, but her poised demeanor left an impression even before she spoke.

Her face looked very familiar, and to avoid embarrassing myself or making her uncomfortable, I let my mind sift through shades of memory. It was as if I was sorting through flickering negatives or cracked Polaroids, each image seeking clarity, trying to place this face in the context of my past.

This couldn't be, I thought, but my curiosity refused to let the notion go. I couldn't shake the feeling of knowing her from somewhere. My mind raced, flipping through past moments like a deck of cards, wondering if I was imagining things.

"Mr. Jacob's," she said, "Are you, Mr. Jacob Foster?"

I looked up.

All her photos were now personified in the flesh.

"Hi, my name is Brianna. I've heard a lot about you from my mother."

"I'm sorry, young lady. Do we know each other?"

"My mother's name is Tina. She often talks about this one house party where you stood up for her after some guys called her out of her name. She said she never forgot how you made her feel valued and respected."

"Oh, yes. I do remember."

"It's funny how life works, isn't it?" Her voice was delightful.

"I am assuming you are her daughter?"

"Yes."

I prepared internally to answer any questions she had, but the moment broke when her name was called for her order. It was funny how things worked for me now that I was in my father's position at the Diner, except she was more pleasant and receptive.

My foot shook nervously under the table as she returned.

"May I have a seat?"

"Of course."

Placing her coffee on the table and her backpack on the floor, she made herself comfortable in front of me.

"So, what brings you to *Barnes and Noble*?" I asked as an ice breaker.

"I am here to meet some classmates for a class

project."

"Oh. Very interesting. What class may I ask?"

"It's a business class. I've just started classes towards my MBA, and we are already swamped with group projects."

"Stick with it. It will all pay off after a while."

"So, Mr. Jacob. May I ask you a question I've always had in the back of my mind?"

"Sure."

"Do you think people are meant to stay in our lives, or just pass through to shape us?"

Before I could answer, she smiled, gathered her things.

"Mr. Jacob, it was such a pleasure to meet you."

"Brianna! Come on," her group called as they entered the bookstore, walking to their designated study area in an open space with soft couches, ironically, between the family and self-help book aisle.

I watched her, as a father would a daughter. A glimpse of what could have been.

Chapter 35

Saturday morning. Game time.

The morning began gently, a thin haze of dew clinging to the grass. By noon, the forecast promised heat, just in time for Zion's soccer tournament.

I encouraged Lisa to take the morning for herself. A few uninterrupted hours without the usual weekend rush. It wasn't often she allowed that kind of pause, and the gratitude in her eyes told me she needed it more than she let on. She had been carrying a lot lately... steadily. This small freedom loosened something in her.

Zion, on the other hand, was all motion.

His excitement filled the garage as we loaded his soccer bag, a folding lawn chair, and a cooler into the trunk.

He talked nonstop about the game, positions, plays, who he hoped to score against, his grin wide and unguarded. Our family was scheduled to bring snacks and drinks that morning, and Lisa, ever prepared, had already texted me the list.

We made a quick stop at the grocery store, grabbing what the parent sign-up required, then headed back home before leaving for the field.

Inside, Lisa stood in the kitchen wearing her favorite robe and slippers, a sleeping mask pushed up on her head like ski goggles as she poured herself a cup of coffee. She already looked rested, or just hopeful.

"Enjoy the game," she said with a smile. "Bring us a win, Zion."

She planned to spend the morning reading a novel she'd been saving and soaking in a long bath, small luxuries she rarely claimed. This was my time to show up. She'd given me that space.

As we buckled in, I glanced at him. "Ready to score some goals, champ?"

"I can't wait."

"I'm excited to see it in action. You've been practicing hard this week."

"Yeah," he said, then hesitated. "I'm a little nervous."

"Me too," I admitted. "That usually means it matters."

The garage door lowered behind us as we pulled away.

As we pulled into the parking lot, crowded with cars and bustling with cheering parents, the soccer tournaments were in full swing. It wasn't just any ordinary Saturday morning tournament; it was the annual city championships, a tradition in our family for years. The significance of this event was palpable, as every team member, family member, and coach had been eagerly expecting it. Zion's team, the Eagles, were defending champions, having clinched the title for the past two years, and there was an invigorating mix of hope and pressure among us. Other family members arrived, filled with excitement.

Zion jumped out of the car to talk to one of his teammates, leaving his friend's father and me alone to unload. As I awkwardly juggled a lawn chair, cooler, and an avalanche of post-game snacks, I couldn't help but chuckle at the classic 'parent pack mule' moment.

Hearing the shuffling of his soccer bag and the clashing of my lawn chair against the cooler, now packed with ice, drinks, and their required snacks after the game.

Zion turned towards me. 'Sorry, Dad, I guess I got carried away."

"That's okay, son," I said, smiling at him. "I know you are excited to see your teammates. But I could use a *little* help at least with your soccer bag. I think I can manage everything else after you close the trunk."

Zion said a momentary goodbye to his teammate as we found a clear spot near the field's goal line, close to patches of brownish grass that had been cut too low.

Let the Game Begin

The game tightened into something sharp and breathless. *Sharks* versus *Eagles*... championship point. The score knotted at 3–3.

The ball broke loose at midfield and found Zion's feet. He cut toward the goal, eyes up, body leaning forward. One of the Sharks, known for playing just past the edge, closed in fast. Seeing the chance, he swung high for the ball. Too high.

His cleat caught Zion's knee. Zion went down hard, the whistle shrilling as the game stalled.

"Come on, ref, that kid's not hurt. He's faking. They are using him to hold up the game."

The voice heckled from across the field, sharp and

dismissive.

I was already running, the grass blurring beneath my feet. Zion's coach knelt beside him as I dropped down, my world narrowing to my son's face.

"You okay, son?"

Everything else faded: the crowd, the shouting, the accusation still ringing in my head.

"I'm okay, Dad," he said, steady but shaken.

The crowd applauded as he stood, brushing grass from his shorts. I clapped too, but the comment stayed lodged inside me, replaying louder each time.

Zion was awarded a penalty kick.

He stood alone at the spot, the field hushed. His shoulders lifted with a breath; eyes locked on the goal. The weight of the moment pressed down on him, winning point, everyone watching.

He took his steps and struck the ball clean. For a split second, the world held still.

Then the net rippled.

The field exploded. Cheers. Arms in the air. Teammates rushed him from every direction.

"All luck," the same parent muttered nearby. "They must've paid the ref."

I turned.

Zion was already looking at me.

Not scared. Not proud.

Watching.

My body moved before my mind caught up. My steps felt heavy, familiar, the old war-fighting nature pulling toward confrontation, tightening my chest. My hand curled into a fist, then slowly opened. I knew what Zion was measuring at that moment. Not the man in front of me.

Me.

I stopped in front of the heckling parent. "Hey," I said evenly. "Good game."

I held out my hand.

He looked at it, then passed me. Without a word, he turned away, gathering his things, ushering his family toward the parking lot.

I let my hand fall.

When I turned back, Zion was smiling, small, uncertain, but there. I walked toward him, catching the tail end of his coach's congratulations as the team clustered together, laughing, shouting, alive.

Zion met my eyes once more. This time, he nodded.

Chapter 36

The Taste of Victory

Zion was excited with his score-winning trophy in hand. After loading everything into the trunk of the car, Zion's teammates and their parents congratulated him for a job well done. Seeing his eyes as bright as the noonday sun made the moment truly special, reflecting his pure joy.

"What a game, Dad!" Zion exclaimed.

"You were incredible! I've never been prouder."

"I practiced a lot. Coach had some great tips, but I owe it to the team."

"Mark's sprint and perfect pass made it happen, even after I got tripped."

"Mark is cool like that. He's one of the best players on the team!"

"Your mother is certainly going to enjoy how great you did today."

"She told me to bring her a win. I couldn't let her down!"

"Stay humble, little man," I teased as we stopped for burgers. I told him he could order anything he wanted, just don't tell Mom.

We sat down by the window with our trays. The inviting aroma of juicy burgers and fries greeted us, making for a pleasant end to the sports day.

Zion was down to half of his burger when he came up for air and asked, "Dad, were you mad when you heard that man from the other side saying those mean things about me during the game?"

"Of course. The old me wanted to react, but I didn't. I thought about our family first."

Zion thought for a second, the spark of excitement in his eyes dimming as he reflected on my words. He remained silent, sipping his drink and clearly considering what I had said. After a moment, he returned to his burger, now more thoughtful than before.

***

As soon as we pulled into the garage, Zion jumped out of the car, proudly carrying his soccer trophy into the house. I followed, eager to see him share his excitement with Lisa, who had been enjoying a rare quiet afternoon. She wore her favorite jeans and her college halter top, looking relaxed as she read her novel. Her peaceful afternoon was about to turn into a lively celebration.

She was startled as he ran in so fast; she had barely enough time to stand as he hugged her and showed her his trophy.

"Well, my, my, my, what do we have here?"

Lisa set her novel face down on the cozy chair in our home library.

"I did it! I scored the winning goal in our soccer game just like you said."

"I knew you could," Lisa said as Zion handed her the trophy. She looked it over, smiling with delight.

"Honey, did you take pictures of the game?"

"*Uhhh...*" I stammered. "No, but I cheered a lot and was probably too caught up in the game to remember."

"That's okay. Seeing Zion so happy made me feel like I was there."

Zion's eyes lit up as he excitedly retold every play. He acted out his moves, sprinting in place to show how he dribbled past defenders and flapping his arm like a wing when he talked about a missed corner kick. Lisa watched him with amazement and affection, sometimes laughing at his lively storytelling.

His voice grew more excited as he described the final moments, waving his hands to show how the ball flew toward the goal. Lisa's nods and smiles encouraged him, and her gasp at the big moment made it feel even more real. I was amazed as he shared details I hadn't noticed, and I saw how her attention brought his stories to life.

"Do you think I can give my trophy to Grandma Ella, after she is released from the hospital tomorrow?" Zion asked, a hint of concern mixed with hope in his voice. "I want her to know she's my biggest cheerleader, even when she can't be there.

"Of course, son. She would love that," I said in agreement.

"C'mon, son, let's finish unloading the car before we forget."

After we unloaded his soccer bag and the lawn chair, we emptied the extra water from the cooler onto the driveway, then went back inside.

"Zion, before you shower and change, remember to take your cleats out of your bag and clean them outside.

"Yes, sir," Zion said.

"So how was your day?" I turned to Lisa.

"It was much needed. But the house was so quiet," Lisa said, her voice full of longing. She looked around the room, her eyes settling on the empty spot next to her on the couch. "I miss the sounds of you two," she went on, her voice softer. "Even the chaos makes the house feel alive. When you're not here, it's different. It feels like something is missing." She smiled warmly, but her eyes shone with genuine emotion.

"We missed you, too, and we are so glad to be home. Although it was just for a few hours."

We both laughed.

Chapter 37

Hospital Release

It had been a week of small, hard-earned victories. But none bigger than this. My mother was coming home.

I usually wore a suit and tie to church, but that morning I chose business casual. I wanted to be ready in case she needed help settling in later that evening.

Zion carried his trophy carefully, rehearsing what he would say to Grandma Ella. Lisa's energy was quieter, hopeful, but thoughtful. My mother's return would shift the rhythm of our home.

We all knew it. After service, we stopped at a restaurant near the hospital for an early dinner before heading over to wait for her release.

When the sliding doors opened, the memory of the night she was rushed to the emergency room hit me hard, flashing lights, uncertainty, the weight of not knowing.

Walking in now felt different.

Grateful.

The air was sterile and chilly as always. The floors had been freshly waxed and shone like glass, reflecting the overhead lights and amplifying the sound of our footsteps as we moved toward the elevator.

Lisa's hand felt cold in mine. Without thinking, I slipped off my jacket and draped it over her shoulders as the elevator doors closed and carried us up to the third floor.

As the elevator doors opened, Zion darted out ahead of us, practically bouncing on his toes. He grinned widely and clutched his trophy tightly against his chest, eyes bright with anticipation.

"Hold on, young man," I called. "Where are you going?"

"I want to show Grandma my trophy!"

Zion looked down in the hallway as if his instinct would guide him.

"Do you even know what room she's in?"

"Nope, but I am sure I can find her.

"Whoa." I placed my hand on his shoulder, stopping him in his tracks.

Lisa stepped out of the elevator last.

For a split second, we had forgotten our chivalry, letting Zion rush ahead of me, while Lisa stood behind me.

She didn't say a word. Just standing there with her arms folded loosely, lips pressed together. I was caught in the middle between boyhood energy and grown-man responsibility.

"Zion," I said gently, kneeling slightly to meet his eyes, "I know you're excited. But there are a few hospital rules you might not know about."

"Like what?"

"Like not overwhelming your grandmother."

"What does that mean?" Zion inquired.

"She's still recovering and we don't want to overexcite her."

"But she really likes my hugs."

I smiled. "I know she does."

I stood and glanced back at Lisa.

"Tell you what. Why don't you and Mom sit in the waiting area, and I'll check to see how Grandma Ella is doing first?"

"Okay, Dad."

I guided him back toward Lisa and leaned in to kiss her cheek.

"I'll be back," I whispered. "And I promise not to spoil your surprise, son."

Zion carefully placed his trophy on the chair beside him.

"Honey," Lisa said softly as I turned around, "try not to stay too long. Let Mother Ella finish signing her paperwork so we can get her out of here because I know how you like to talk."

I nodded and smiled.

As I approached her hospital room, I tapped lightly on the doorframe and stepped inside.

"Mother, are you ready?"

I sent my voice ahead before our eyes met.

"As ready as I will ever be."

Mother sat in a wheelchair near the window as two nurses prepared her discharge paperwork, explaining instructions while organizing her belongings. Her purse rested on her lap;

her coat folded neatly beside her.

"Ms. Foster, I just need you to sign here," a nurse handed her a clipboard with a release form and a pen.

Pages shuffled, signatures repeated.

When the nurse finished, my mother handed the pen back and smiled faintly. I reached for the wheelchair, ready to roll her out.

"Sir," the nurse said gently, stopping my hand. "Hospital policy, we'll escort her out. But if you carry her belongings and pull the car around to the front, that would be great."

I nodded. "Of course."

I stepped back into the hallway.

Zion stood, with a trophy in hand, ready to recite the speech we all knew because he rehearsed it so much. The moment he laid eyes on me, he knew that Grandma Ella was not too far behind.

By now, Zion's excitement spilled over to other families as they looked on in admiration of his anticipation.

"Grandma!"

Zion yelled as she turned the corner in the wheelchair.

The nurse wheeling my mother smiled but never compromised my mother's safety, slowing the wheelchair just in time to give me a buffer to tell him not to run at half speed.

"Zion, be careful." Lisa declared, knowing his hugs all too well.

"Look, Grandma! This is for you!"

"What do we have here?" Mother replied with a returned twinkle in her eyes. "That's my boy!"

Zion and my mother's bond was reunited. Though I could not explain, it was something very special.

"Hold on to your trophy, son. We must get her into the car first, then you can give it to her."

"He's just excited. He's okay." My mother said in his defense.

While Lisa gave my mother a tender embrace, Zion, on the other hand, was unfettered, rattling off his story of victory as he walked backward, talking a mile a minute.

"Wait, wait, son! Catch your breath and breathe."

Lisa and I chuckled as I struggled to press the elevator button with my mother's belongings; Lisa obliged.

As the elevator opened on the first floor, I turned to Zion. "You and your mom wait here with grandma until I pull the car around."

I could hear faint conversations between Lisa and my mother as they were catching up on her hospital stay and how she was feeling.

The warm smile of Zion as my mother held her special trophy, like a bouquet of roses, from her grandson.

Chapter 38

Home Sweet Home

My mother was finally released from the hospital, and happiness should have been the only thing filling the car. Yet I couldn't help wondering whether Lisa was already calculating the adjustments ahead, just when our family had settled into a rhythm that felt steady.

My mother carefully held Zion's trophy in her lap, admiring it as he narrated every detail of the game from the back seat. The two of them talked like old friends who had been reunited.

I glanced at Lisa in the rearview mirror, hoping to understand her quiet mood. For most of the ride, her gaze was distant, fixed on the window as if she were lost in thought.

Present. But her mind seemed far away, detached from our laughter. I cracked a few *dad-jokes*, hoping to pull her back. Everyone laughed.

Except her.

She smiled, but it was restrained and distant, the guarded smile of someone holding back what they're feeling. I tried to imagine myself in her place.

Doctor visits were ahead: follow-ups, adjustments

Time.

Time that might once have belonged to my wife, now redirected.

The hours that would have been ours might now be spent caring for my mother. To Lisa, that change would be real and fair.

Still, I was assuming too much. It had been a long week for her. Maybe work had drained her. Or maybe she was simply tired. Still, something in her countenance had changed.

***

When we pulled into the driveway, my mother insisted on going straight inside. The hospital week had exhausted her, though she tried not to show it.

I grabbed a courtesy hospital tote bag and slung it over my shoulder. Zion carried the other, its strap a small reminder of responsibility. My mother held Zion's trophy, reassuring him his gift wasn't forgotten.

Lisa and I walked beside her, steadying her until we reached the front door.

My mother's home was always modest but intentional.

Every chair is placed with care. Every surface respected.

Familiarity greeted us as the door opened, like an embrace.

She paused at the threshold.

Relief softened her face. Gratitude flickered in her eyes. She inhaled deeply, as if reclaiming something borrowed from her. At once, she began noting what needed dusting.

Resilient. Already reclaiming her space.

"Grandma," Zion asked eagerly, "where are you going to put your trophy?"

"In my room," she replied. "So, I can wake up and see it every day."

Zion nearly bounced with excitement. Mother settled into her favorite chair.

"You can place it wherever you like in my room," she told him.

Lisa sat nearby.

"Mother Ella, is there anything we can do?" she asked.

"I'm quite alright, Suga. Thank you."

"I'll put your bags in your room, Mom," I said.

She slipped off her slippers, leaned back, and exhaled slowly. Home. Finally.

Seeing that my mother was content and well enough to be alone, as she preferred, we said our goodbyes and set out on our journey home.

Chapter 39

The Measure of a Man

The silence in the car wasn't tense. It was thoughtful. Lisa was always honest, so I didn't press her. I waited. Zion, in the back seat, smiled gently, still enjoying his memory of my mother.

The radio played softly beneath our thoughts.

When we arrived home, the transition from reflective silence to the comfort of familiar routines was subtle. Each of us instinctively sought our own ways to unwind, the emotional weight shifting as we returned to our own space.

Lisa kicked off her shoes near the door and loosened her

hair. I opened the refrigerator as if something new might have appeared since we left. Zion disappeared into the living room, television already humming to life... normalcy.

After the house quieted, I asked Lisa to join me in the library. I set the mood with lights, a fireplace, pillows, and a blanket. She smiled.

"So, what's the special occasion?"

"No occasion. Just time." She studied me and sat beside me.

"Long day, I know. But what's on your heart?" I asked.

"A lot."

"I'm listening."

Lisa inhaled slowly before speaking. "Jacob, you know I love your mother like she's my own."

I shifted closer, giving her my full attention.

"But I'm worried," she continued carefully. "Not because I don't care, but because we worked so hard to build stability. And now that I feel we are finally here... everything might shift again."

I took her hand.

"I've been thinking the same thing," I said honestly. "I

feel the same."

"I don't want to sound selfish."

"You don't."

"It just feels like everything is happening at once." No accusation in her voice, only concern. "What do you suggest?" I asked, not to challenge her but to honor her perspective.

She shook her head softly. "I don't know if there's a perfect answer."

We let the silence sit. It wasn't heavy, just honest, a shared space for both our uncertainties. I wasn't focused on fixing anything at that moment. I only wanted her to feel heard.

"I saw it in the car. It's a lot. That's why we have each other. We'll figure it out."

"We always do." She leaned in.

We relaxed on the couch and in front of the fireplace. I traced her arm, kissed her head, breathing in her scent.

For a moment, the world felt steady.

"Babe, there's something on my heart too." She looked up, calm.

"When should Zion meet Keith?" Her steady expression surprised me.

"What do you think?" she asked softly. "Or better yet… how do you feel?"

I paused. That needed honesty.

"I believe in second chances. Holding onto the past doesn't help."

"But?"

"I've never been here before. I don't know what it should feel like."

She nodded.

"Have you forgiven him? Or is there still something?"

I searched within myself.

"I don't think it's resentment," I said carefully. "Maybe caution."

"That's fair."

Silence returned, but this time it carried understanding.

"I trust you," she said finally. "You'll know when the time is right."

I looked at her.

Really looked at her.

I felt the weight of gratitude.

"I love you."

"I know."

We stayed there, wrapped in warmth and quiet assurance, until sleep found us both.

Chapter 40

Where You Come From

I cancelled Saturday morning workout plans with Ralph and decided to take Zion to the park instead.

The weather was fair, slightly overcast. The clouds weren't perfect, but not enough to spoil basketball with Zion.

At Zion's door, I hesitated, hand on the frame, listening to him get ready. I hadn't told him much. In that stillness, I could feel questions rising, unspoken, just beneath the surface. Some part of me braced for the day he'd ask about my own father, the story I always kept out of reach, folded into our routines.

Raised in a fatherless home, I remembered flashes of the empty places at my birthdays and games. That absence taught me to expect less and shaped my understanding of trust. It reflected how I felt that morning. I wondered how best to tell Zion about who my father was.

"Are you ready, son?" I called, grabbing my keys.

"Yes, sir."

We both said our goodbyes to Lisa before we left.

Only a few players were on the court, having more conversations than playing. The chain link fence rattled from a missed shot by a lone player as we stepped onto the court.

Zion dribbled in front of me while I stretched, careful not to pull a muscle. Our energy levels were night and day. Once I finished, Zion passed me the ball. I tucked it under my arm and switched gears.

Feet wide.

Eyes up.

I transitioned into coach-dad mode.

"Now, son, this is a serious game that requires technique and skill, you understand?" I said.

"Yes, Dad."

Zion sighed, preparing for another long-winded story, sensing I had already stepped onto my soapbox.

"This is not just a basketball, but in streetball, we call this, the *rock*."

"The *rock*?"

Zion's face appeared confused.

"The *rock*!"

I bounced the ball sternly on the ground, dribbling with precision between my legs a few times, mixed with quick head fakes.

"Do you see my *skillz*, son?"

"Yeah, I see them, Dad," Zion said with a chuckle, voice tinged with sarcasm.

I passed the ball to Zion, dribbling in front of me, focused and determined; it returned faithfully to his hand each time it struck the pavement.

"Keep your elbow in," I coached.

He adjusted mid-motion. The shot fell clean through the net.

I stood amazed.

"Okay, son. I see your little *skillz*," *I said* heartily.

He turned with a grin. "I'm getting there."

"You are."

We kept firing shots.

Swish.

Rim.

Chase.

Correct.

Reset.

Our rhythm needed no words; the give-and-go said enough.

"Did you ever play like this with your dad?"

The question floated between us, lingering as if it had been waiting.

My heart dropped as I realized the question I'd been dreading had finally arrived, stirring up old pain and vulnerability.

"Not really," I said evenly.

He stopped dribbling.

"Why not?"

"Unfortunately, he wasn't around."

Zion studied me, curiosity in his gaze, not pity or confusion.

"Did that make you mad?"

"It did," I admitted. "For a long time… but I managed."

He nodded slowly, absorbing the idea of growing up fatherless.

The wind brushed past us, carrying the faint scent of cut grass.

He bounced the ball again and took a shot, but shot an airball, just within my reach.

"Where is he now?"

"Around."

"You talk to him?"

I was silent for a moment, contemplating how to answer.

"Not often."

"Why do you never talk about him? I tell my friends stories about you *all* the time," Zion said.

I stepped closer.

"To be honest, I don't know. My story of having a father is much different than yours. Unfortunately, one, I am not too proud of."

I paused, searching for the right words.

For years, I kept my past to myself to protect you from pain and confusion. I didn't want what I carried to spill into your life or shape your ideas of a father.

He considered that.

Then, gently, "Can I meet him?"

I felt the weight of the question, heavier than before, but noticed it brought a new sense of acceptance rather than the old sting of regret.

My mother always said that running from something only made it heavier. Facing it doesn't make it disappear, but it stops it from chasing you.

"You want to?" I asked.

Zion shrugged lightly. "I think so. I *wanna* know where you come from."

There was no accusation in his voice. No expectation.

Just openness.

And in that openness, I saw something I hadn't had at his age, the ability to forgive before fully understanding.

"If we do that," I said, "we need to move slowly."

He nodded. "Okay."

We returned to the game, but something had shifted. The tension was replaced by a new sense of awareness between us. He wasn't trying to fill a gap but to understand his roots. I realized, despite my intimidation, that I was no longer afraid of him discovering them.

***

As we walked into the house, kitchen aromas drew us in. I recognized the smell as we approached Lisa, who stood at the stove, preparing her mother's signature honey-curry-glazed chicken and rice.

"Babe, this food smells delicious," I said, hugging her from behind while she stirred the skillet. Zion echoed.

"I just felt nostalgic this morning for some reason, and I knew you two would come home with hungry stomachs. *Unless* you stopped for *fast food?*" Lisa asked, raising an eyebrow.

"Of course not, *right*, Zion?" I replied.

"You're *right*, Dad!" Zion chimed in with a huge wink.

"So, who won the game?" Lisa asked, noticing our sweat from playing.

"We just shot some hoops." I replied before Zion

interrupted inadvertently.

"Mom. Did you know that basketball is also called a *rock*?" Zion said.

"A *rock*?" Lisa paused from stirring, playing into the story. "Who told you that?"

"Dad. He said it's called shooting a rock when it comes to streetball," Zion responded.

Lisa's eyes darted in my direction. I shrugged my shoulders and smiled.

"He taught me a few more things, too."

Zion tried to spin the basketball on his finger, grinned, and blurted out of thin air, "Mom, have you ever met Dad's father?"

Lisa's face turned flush; I widened my eyes, and the investigation had begun.

The room quieted.

Lisa turned the stove down before facing us fully. The wooden spoon rested against the skillet's edge.

She didn't look startled.

Just attentive.

"I haven't," she said gently.

Zion blinked. "You *haven't*?"

She shook her head. "No."

His eyes shifted to me.

"You never wanted Mom to meet him?"

Zion's question, though innocent, felt confrontational, but justified.

"It never felt necessary," I said.

Lisa didn't interrupt that. She folded her hands in front of her.

"What's he like?" Zion asked, curiosity was evident.

I considered the question carefully.

"He's… a man who made choices."

Zion waited.

"Good choices?" Zion prompted.

"Not all of them," I replied.

My wife stepped closer, her voice steady. "People can grow," she said softly.

Zion looked at her and then back at me. "Can I meet him?" he asked again. The question felt different now, not merely curious, but intentional.

She didn't rush to answer.

She handed the question to me, as if wondering if I had come to a resolution since our last conversation on the floor in front of the library.

"I'm okay with it, but I would like to have a talk with him first," I responded.

"How do you feel about that?" Lisa asked Zion.

"I just want to know," he replied. "I want to know where you come from, Dad."

There it was again—not filling a gap, but tracing roots.

Her expression softened. "If this happens," she said carefully, "it will happen slowly."

She ironically echoed what I had told him at the park. It was reassuring to know we were on the same page.

I nodded in agreement, and Zion accepted that.

"Yes, ma'am," Zion said.

The tension faded, replaced by a gentle relief that settled between us, making the house feel lighter—with a shared understanding calmly present.

My wife returned to the stove. Zion set the table. The house felt quieter than before. Not heavy, just aware.

***

Later that night, after Zion went to his room, Lisa and I sat on the couch.

The house had settled into its evening rhythm.

"You knew this day would come," she said.

"I did. But it came sooner than I expected."

"And?"

I leaned back, thinking.

"I don't feel anger," I admitted. "That's new."

She studied my face.

"Do you feel ready?"

"For what?"

"To see him as he is."

That question lingered.

"I think so," I said. "But this isn't just about me anymore."

"No," she agreed.

"It's about what we model."

She nodded slowly.

"You've never spoken about him with bitterness," she said. "Even when you could have."

"That was intentional."

"I know."

Her hand rested lightly on mine.

"I trust you," she said.

"I don't want Zion carrying anything that isn't his," I said.

"He won't," she replied. "Because you won't hand it to him."

Her words settled in me, leaving me both reflective and relieved, aware of the comfort that came with her support.

"I'll call him tomorrow."

Lisa nodded.

Chapter 41

Clarity

I wasn't ready, and I didn't want to be, to call Keith the next afternoon. I had so many conversations tucked away: Accusations I'd practiced, old grievances I'd refined over the years. But this call wasn't about any of that. This was about Zion.

He answered on the third ring.

"Jacob."

"Zion asked about you," I said.

Silence followed. Not confusion, recalibration.

"What did you tell him?"

"The truth."

"He wants to meet you."

The conversation deepened.

"I don't want to disrupt anything," Keith said.

"You won't," I replied. "We'll handle this right, correctly."

A pause.

"I can make up for lost time. The settlement of my case is coming through soon. I could…"

"This isn't about money," I said sternly.

He stopped.

"The money won't replace absence," I continued evenly. "It won't replace birthdays. It won't erase what you did to my mother. It won't untangle what prison took or what you chose before it. Zion doesn't need compensation. He needs honesty."

There was no defensiveness.

No argument.

"I understand," he said.

"We'll meet first. Just you and me."

"I understand."

"Soon."

"Okay."

The call ended without apology or closure… just an

agreement.

For once, that was enough.

Two Days Later

We met at the same Diner. The booths were half-full, filled
with the usual scent of coffee and grease, along with a faintly
sweet note.

He stood when I approached.

"You look well," he said.

"I am." We sat.

"Zion wants to meet you."

His eyes dropped, then met mine.

"I don't deserve that."

"No," I said. "You don't."

It was just the truth.

"But this isn't about deserving," I continued. "It's about
clarity."

He nodded.

"If he asks why, you weren't there, you answer honestly."

"I will."

"No excuses."

"I won't."

"No rewriting."

"I won't."

I held his gaze, searching for defensiveness, pride,

volatility, anything I remembered from the accounts my mother never fully told but never had to. There was none.

"I built stability without you," I said. "He has consistency. He has presence. He has safety."

"I can see that," he replied calmly.

"And if this disrupts that, I step in."

"You should."

It was strange how calm it was. Not forgiveness. Not reconciliation. Just boundaries recognized.

"I'm not bringing you into his life as a replacement," I said. "He already has a father."

"I know," he answered. "And you've done well."

When I stood, he stood too.

"Jacob."

I paused.

"I made the wrong choice." He said, apologetically. I let his words hang in the space between us.

"I'm not asking for anything," he added.

"I know," I said.

And I did.

"I'll let you know when he's ready."

"Thank you."

I nodded once and left.

***

Later that day, when I pulled into the driveway, I didn't sit in the car this time. There was no heaviness waiting to be gathered before stepping inside. Lisa looked up from the couch.

"How did it go?"

"It went the way it needed to." She searched my face for strain. "You, okay?"

"Yes." And I meant it.

Zion appeared in the hallway. "You met him?"

"I did."

He examined me carefully.

"Was he nervous?"

"A little."

Zion nodded, considering that. "When do I meet him?"

"Tomorrow evening," I said.

He smiled, not wide, not ecstatic, just steady. Something in me settled fully; the past was no longer advancing, only standing still.

Chapter 42

Where it Ends

We met at the park.

It was neutral ground, sky unbound, no walls trapping old echoes. Zion stood beside me, hands deep in his hoodie pockets. He seemed calm, watchful, mature enough to know silence holds meaning. Keith approached without hesitation, not rushed or uncertain, but purposeful in every step. For a moment, the three of us shared that space.

No one spoke; no one withdrew.

"Hi," Zion said first.

"Hello," Keith replied. They shook hands. Keith's grip was

measured, firm without being forceful, careful without being weak.

We sat together on the bench facing the basketball court, the conversation shifting naturally as Zion didn't circle the subject.

"Why weren't you there?" he asked.

Keith exhaled, neither defensive nor theatrical… just a man reaching for the truth, unpolished.

"I hurt your grandmother when I was younger," he said. "I was angry and made wrong choices." He paused, letting the words settle. "After that, I went to prison for something I didn't do. Both are true."

No excuses. No rearranging facts.

Zion heard this, his face unreadable as he watched Keith. He didn't frown or smile, just stayed still, eyes searching Keith for meaning.

"Did you say sorry to my Grandma Ella for being mean to her?" he asked carefully.

"Yes," Keith said. "More than once."

"Did she forgive you?"

A small silence settled among us, each of us feeling the honesty that lingered.

"No," he answered. "I don't think she did."

Honesty hung in the air, unprotected.

Zion nodded.

"My dad's not like that," he said gently.

His words struck me with tenderness I didn't feel worthy of. I knew my flaws, how I had stumbled before, but in his eyes, I was steadier than I believed.

"I don't think he would ever hurt my mom that way." Zion continued.

Keith's jaw tightened imperceptibly. Then he spoke.

"I know," he said. "He's better than I was back then."

There was no envy in his words, no bitterness, just recognition.

After a silent moment, Zion stood up.

"You want to see my shot?" he asked.

Keith looked at him the way someone regards something delicate he knows he cannot claim.

"Yes," he said.

Zion stepped onto the court, dribbled twice, and set his feet. The ball rose cleanly, spinning against the pale sky, dropping through the net with a soft snap.

Keith clapped without performing, just enough to acknowledge the moment.

I watched them both, feeling a cautious hope that nothing would break the brief peace between us.

The moment held firm.

Zion retrieved the ball and passed it to me.

"Your turn, Dad," he said.

I caught it.

The leather felt familiar, solid, and certain in my hands.

For a moment, we stood together in stillness, the past present but not dominating, the present steady, the future unclaimed. The ball rested in my palm.

What had happened before would always be true.

But it no longer owned the air we were breathing.

I dribbled once, set my feet, and shot.

The ball arced higher than needed before falling clean through the net.

There was no applause, no announcement, just the quiet certainty of something finding its place.

Zion grinned.

Keith nodded once.

The game wasn't over, but it was no longer about *what had been missed*

Acknowledgments

God be Praised.

I want to express my heartfelt gratitude to my wife, Viola, for her love and unwavering encouragement, which have been the foundation of my journey. I am also profoundly thankful to my children, who inspire me daily to lead by example, and I appreciate their patience during the countless hours I dedicated to this work.

My thanks extend to my mother, my late father, my siblings, and my extended family for their support. I am grateful to my pastor, Bishop Dr. Mikel, and Lady Debra Brown, whose faith and leadership guide me. To the Joy Center family, your encouragement has been invaluable.

Thank you to everyone who has played a significant role in my life, as well as to the readers and supporters of "At a Mirror's Glance," "Letting Go of the Perfect," and my future books.

God bless you and thank you!.